THE REUNION TRILOGY

IMOGENE NIX

Print ISBN: 978-0-9954182-7-1

PART I

War's End

Forced apart by war five years ago, Renjiro and Selina have another chance at love. Can they make it work or does fate have other plans?

Without the citizenship of the Federation, Indy pilot Selina Codecko is treated like a second-class citizen. When she gets caught up in a bar brawl she's arrested and finds herself in the hands of the Justice Officers.

Renjiro Ito has dreamed of Selina for five long years. As the Commander of the Justice Officers, the plight of this one woman will turn his life upside down.

But there's more going on than just the fate of one woman—there's a seething underbelly that wants to destroy their newly expanded Federation. The chances of a future together are slim, but they'll take any chances that come their way. Will it be enough?

Chapter 1

Selina's finger tensed on the throttle of the tiny craft as she guided it into the moon base waiting pattern.

Moon Base 703 had the reputation of being difficult to navigate without incidents, but Selina knew she didn't have the luxury of damaging this craft. If she made any mistake Ashford, who was a cantankerous boss, would have no problem blaming her. He'd made it clear after the last scrape she'd unwittingly fallen into that she had no more chances left. He'd let her go without qualms.

She had no home, no family, and nowhere to retreat to. So she couldn't afford to make a mistake. Ever.

"Better get this right, Selina." The cabin was tiny , but the sound of her words still reverberated in it.

"*Sylvie's Dream*, you are cleared for landing on Moon Base 703. Berth A five four on level seven has been cleared for your arrival." The disinterested tones of the moon base traffic officer rattled through the old speaker.

"Affirmative, Moon Base 703. Berth acknowledged. *Sylvie's Dream* will begin entry sequence now." She carefully tapped the details into the keyboard then waited for the navigational unit to settle on the best path.

If it wasn't for the load she was to pick up there, she would have happily avoided this port. She hated busy moon bases; mainly because they reminded her of the days she'd spent flying during the war, when any port like this spelled danger. Intrigue had been everywhere and one misstep... Well, remembering wouldn't help.

The independent planets had lost the war and were subsumed by the acquisitive Federation. She had lost all her rights to citizenship because she'd been a fighter pilot for the other side. All that stopped her from being banished was her skill as a pilot. Ashford had taken advantage of the need in the Federation for well trained freighter pilots, claiming that they were necessary for the continuation of commerce.

She brushed away the memories best forgotten with the ease of experience.

Vehicles passed her, lumbering space tankers and the new, highly maneuverable luxury shuttles. They passed close, and on more than one occasion, she gritted her teeth as the proximity alarms blared.

The berth lay ahead. The massive gray doors imprinted with the designation in fluorescent yellow confirmed her location. With care, she propelled the aging Centura G-9 into position and the docking clamps met the ship with a clunk and thud. From the side viewport, it was easy to watch the great doors open wide and the clamps pull the ship into the berth. The cavernous space within brightly lit as the lighting shone on the craft.

"*Sylvie's Dream*, power down your systems and set brakes." Another voice, this one low and melodic, gave the instructions.

Her fingers flew over the controls before she depressed the comms button. "*Sylvie's Dream* acknowledges. Systems powering down and brakes are set." With a sigh, she removed her finger from the button.

For a moment, she stayed in her chair, slumped in the creaky padded seat. She reached for her safety belts and unclipped them. They retracted with a hiss and she stood, letting the aches of long hours in the command seat wash off. Then she reached out, grabbing her identity tags and slipping them over her head. She had no standing in the Federation and it was a crime for her to wander anywhere without her information disks. If she was caught out of bounds and they scanned the data chip embedded in her arm, they'd throw her into the prison system.

Even the vague memory of Federation jails left her shivering. It wasn't something she would choose to relive. Not after her experience after a drunken night out. Federation justice officers had been clear—do it again and be banished. *Life sucks sometimes*, she thought.

Selina headed for the door, the clanking of her no-nonsense boots echoing in the corridor, and she reached for the lever. The door slid open with a loud grind and she entered the airlock. The second door required a passcode which she quickly tapped in; it too opened and the aging hinges creaked. On the other side stood a contingent of Federation officials. Waiting. She hated this bit.

"Present your data chip for verification."

Silently, she extended her arm, waiting as they waved the wand over. The quiet beep told her they had the details they sought.

"Present your credentials."

She unclipped the tags hanging at her neck.

They scanned those too then nodded, handing them

back. "You are confined to levels seven, eight, and nine. You should check the public announcement daily and, if required, present yourself to the indentures office by o-seven hundred moon base time. Failure to do so will result in immediate detention. Do you understand these instructions?"

"I do."

The man opposite her smiled in a condescending manner, one she had almost become used to, as he held out a bright pink tag. Anyone who saw it would know she held no official status. She accepted it wordlessly and clipped it to the identity lanyard. The routine was just that, routine. But she still hated the obvious color tag these moon bases used. They were so...*noticeable*.

"Failure to present same tag on request—"

Selina nodded. "Will result in immediate detention. I understand."

He blinked and looked more closely at her before grimacing. "Then you may continue your business." Just like that he turned with a squeak of his boots on the plascrete floor and left her standing there.

She slowly made her way down the ramp to meet with the hard-bodied men waiting. They sized her up, their eyes shining as they attempted to work out whether she'd be willing to undertake a liaison. But as with every other base and depot she had flown into, they held no interest. No man had. Not for a long time.

"Selina Codecko. Captain of the *Sylvie's Dream*." She held out her hand and accepted the shake of the man closest. His callused hand gripped hers firmly. "I'll be loading parts for the Orlach sector in the next day or so."

One of the men raised an eyebrow. "That's a long, lonely run for a single woman." Selina held her ground, meeting his eyes. A bland smile bloomed and she knew it held no invitation to these men. "Maybe, but it's my next run. The ship will require replenishing of food stock, the oxygen tanks inspected and refilled, and the same for the water tanks."

The man who had done all the speaking so far nodded. "Fine. It's a—"

"Centura G-9. Old, but an efficient workhorse."

The man scratched his head. "Fine. Me and the boys will attend to that. You'd better head to level eight and see if there is any accommodation left. They don't let the captains remain onboard here." His gruff words carried an unspoken warning. Those without status were fair game, so play wisely.

Thank you hovered on her lips, but she dismissed the words. Those words could be construed as gratitude and she couldn't afford to be beholden to anyone. She'd lived too long by her wits. Now wasn't the time to forget them.

***

"Sir, we have another individual without status. A Captain Codecko, flying *Sylvie's Dream*. The ship is currently berthed in A five four on level seven."

Renjiro Ito accepted the data chip and was about to place it on the pile with others for perusal, when he stopped and speared the official with a look. "The captain is here for how long?" Many of the other status-less travelers stayed less than a full lunar cycle on the moon base, so by the time he checked their details, they had already left. But if they were going to be there longer... Well, he would check their background. In his position as the Federation 's civil defense commander for the region, he had to ensure the safety of the people in his care.

Many of those without status still held enduring grudges against the Federation. The Indy governments had never explained the necessity to be folded into their united systems. Those disenfranchised by their integration had just blindly fought the Federation. Many of the ground troops who had survived the bitter but brief war had returned to their previous employment.

But the flyers... They hadn't.

No, a proportion had continued with skirmish after skirmish. So the Federation had banished them. After years of bitterness, there were still pockets of resistance. They wanted nothing to do with unity.

While forcible banishment wasn't a perfect outcome—and if Renjiro were honest, he hated it—it was the ruling of the senate. He had to accept their decision.

The female officer flicked through the paperwork that had been generated, pulling Renjiro from his reverie. "I think it is several days. She 's expecting an incoming cargo load to be rerouted to the Orlach sector. She's one of Ashford's people."

Renjiro grunted and slid the chip into the reader. The face that stared back at him was one he knew. He remembered night after night in his dreams, the battle of Seicha Two Seven Seven. Initially, it was a search-and-find mission. It had become more than that once he realized it was also a stronghold for a legion of Indy warriors.

"Where is she currently?" He rasped the request, his heart rate speeding up. If this was her, then he'd seek her out. Ensure she was fine. It was the only way he could thank her for the risks she'd taken during those long days and nights. His hand shook and he shoved it into his pocket to hide his physical response.

"Sir?" The woman in front of him looked confused. "I don't know what you..." Her words died away as he rose.

"Where is she being accommodated?"

"Well, see, there is no current available accommodation on levels seven, eight, or even nine. At this point..." The young officer shrugged. "We don't know where she is at present. We can request all pink tag holders present themselves—"

Renjiro shook his head. "No, that won't be necessary." He reached for the jacket carelessly slung over his seat. "I'm going out. Redirect all transmissions except from my cousin or command."

Her face blanched. "Yes, sir." Her crisp salute was returned as a matter of formality as he left his office, the shushing of the closing door the only sound as he strode into the corridor.

His people were used to him just heading out, and this time he was thankful. He'd been on this moon base for weeks and it always left him feeling jittery and on edge, so he'd walk off his frustrations. Right now, he didn't give a damn about his work or the jitters that sometimes assailed him.

The need to find the woman who'd cared for him was overwhelming, and he fought the memories of her soft touches and the whispery kisses they'd shared. She'd stayed with him for several days before he woke that morning to find her gone. Nothing more than a note filling the place where she'd rested beside him, giving him the coordinates back to his ship, where she'd carefully stashed it. Where she'd found him, alone and injured.

The lift was in front of him and he swiped his

command card. It would override any other commands, and he smiled. He needed to get to level seven. See if she had settled herself in the ship.

The doors whispered open and he strode inside.

Selina propped up the bar, her hand wrapped casually around a beaker of Deluvian wine. It was bitter, but better than the watery ale they were serving in this poor excuse for a bar. As she sipped the brew, she thought over her options. None of the accommodation units on the three levels had vacancies. So, she'd either have to apply for a dispensation and stay on her ship or...

Or what? Where else could she stay?

Selina gulped, letting the liquid slide down her throat. She'd been here five hours. Five long, frustrating hours. The negative emotion rose in her like a thick, oily mass and she closed her eyes for a moment.

As she sat there contemplating the situation, the drunk man on her left made to turn. His movements were ungainly and he jostled her.

"Frick," she muttered. Selina lost her footing and she went down, the beaker still gripped in her hand following her. The wine splashed the man to the right who growled low in his throat.

"Gods damned..." The now wet man on the other side grunted and kicked out angrily. Without thought, she shoved him firmly and he cursed as she caught him in a tender location.

"Bloody Indy bitch." He raised his fisted hand and she turned slightly, noting the change in the atmosphere of the bar. The patrons, many grizzled and looking for an excuse to fight, had risen.

No doubt he's caught sight of the damned pink tag hanging around my neck, she thought. Selina pushed away from the patch of floor where she crouched. She couldn't afford to be caught in the middle of a melee, but already it was too late. The seething mass of patrons roared and shoved, pushed and punched. The bar, she now realized, had been a powder keg, fully primed and ready for the explosion. Unfortunately, even though it wasn't her fault, she had been the detonator.

"I gotta get outta here." As she spoke, her opponent grabbed her hair and tugged. Hard. "Let go of me you damned Fed bastard." The words erupted before she thought and she swung out with her elbow, where she connected with his hand. He let her go as a blow caught her on her jaw and she howled madly. She dodged the fists and feet, pulling herself away from her opponent. She'd moved out of reach when an alarm sounded , capturing the attention of those gathered, and they scattered, pouring out the doors like a rushing torrent of humanity.

The sound confused her as her fogged brain tried to work out what was happening. She cradled her aching knuckles against her chest. She watched as the bar emptied before realizing she'd better get out of there too.

As she reached the door, she was shoved back. Selina fell to the floor with a thud as a number of armed judiciary entered. "Hit the ground and wait for inspection."

She groaned as she assumed a prone position on the floor, her hands clenched behind her back. She dropped her head to the floor. "Nooo, " she whispered, knowing exactly what this meant.

Selina closed her eyes; she felt a pair of hands pull at

the lanyard around her neck. "Sir? We have one here with a pink tag."

She tensed. *Gods damn it!* They were going to take her in. The thought coiled through her, twining like a snake through her belly. But she knew better than to protest. Now was not the time.

When they tugged her upright, she complied with a docility that belied the anger within. She'd been quietly enjoying a drink and hadn't caused the riot. None of this was her fault. But she knew they wouldn't accept that. She was an Indy. Displaced. She had no legal rights.

Geez! If Ashford gets wind of this... Now the coiling mass within her body seized. They'd send her away. She'd be banished.

She felt the metallic clasp of restraints and waited for their next direction. *Perhaps if I follow their instructions—* But she cut the thought short. She knew it wouldn't be that simple.

Beneath the leathery jacket, sweat settled like ice against her skin. She shivered. "Come this way." Rough hands tugged her toward the opening and out onto the concourse.

"Where are you—"

"Be quiet, prisoner."

She swallowed the panic that rose. *Prisoner. Frick.*

The button communicator buzzed once, then again. With a heavy sigh, he tapped it. "Renjiro here."

"Sir, I'm sorry to interrupt, but there has been a riot at one of the bars on level eight." Renjiro closed his eyes. His trip to the berth had been abortive. There was no sign of Captain Codecko, and he'd been considering his next move when the hail came through.

He rolled his shoulders, loosening the tense muscles beneath his uniform. He sucked in a deep breath and responded. "Which bar?"

"The Blue Trader, sir." He knew the bar well. Some of the most hardened freighter captains frequented that establishment.

"I'm on my way." He headed for the lifts, calculating the quickest route even as he overrode the controls. A gaggle of older women frowned at him as the door opened and he stepped within. "Ladies."

They didn't acknowledge the greeting. They did watch him with stony looks and he suppressed a sigh. No doubt the women thought him the reason for any or all of their personal ills. His uniform, which proclaimed him a justice officer, regularly met with that reaction.

As the lift stopped and the doors opened, he heard them whisper. "Damned justice officers. Think they're so special." He ignored their words and strode down the concourse to where a knot of his people waited.

"Sir. We've secured the premises and taken five assailants into custody. One female and four male." The young officer spoke in rapid fire and Renjiro had to stop a smile. The younger officer had been gunning for a promotion for some time.

Renjiro wasn't the person who would be informing him that his application had been approved. Instead Renjiro nodded and waited, knowing the officer would receive all the information he needed soon.

"We believe the riot began with a man jostling the

woman. The eye spies in the ceiling are being observed as we speak. But sir, the woman is a pink tag holder."

His breath fled. *A pink tag holder? It can't be...* He wanted to ask, but fear stopped his words. If it was her, he needed to be prepared. He couldn't stop the process of justice. He didn't have that much authority. And he wouldn't circumvent justice, otherwise his men would know. He would lose face. He couldn't afford that either!

So instead of heading to the lock-up where she was stashed, he straightened his stance, glanced around at the men who waited for his instructions, and made his way inside. Broken furniture was strewn around the shabby establishment in piles. The walls were pitted and scarred. He could detect some new holes, but many had been there a long time. Beakers and tankards were scattered on the floor, and the place stank like a fetid brewery.

The chairs were stained and, in the full light, its dirty glory was obvious. "I can never understand why anyone would drink here."

"It's cheap, sir." His second-in-command stood at his right side. He hadn't heard the man advance, but turned to look at him.

Renjiro grimaced. His family was well placed in the Federation, comfortable enough that credit wasn't an issue. This sort of lifestyle was incomprehensible to him. "Which holding station are the prisoners at?"

"The woman is in Seven Brig one. The men are in Seven Brig three, Ren."

He stilled at the man's use of his name. He knew then there was more, could tell in Jordan's stance.

"She's in need of treatment. Took some good blows. Gave some good ones too, according to the spy eye. But that's not what I need to raise." Jordan stopped, his face flaming, and he looked sideways, as if ensuring no one heard what he was about to say. "It's more that we checked her background. She's a pink tag. Was on some of the same planets as you. Including Seicha Two Seven Seven."

Ren tensed. "Damn!" He couldn't control the outburst as his stomach yawed and pitched. It could be her then. "Just let me handle this, Jordan." Then he strode away.

If it was her, Selina, then he'd have to try to find a way to... But he couldn't think of anything. He had some political clout, but he hadn't ever used it. Not once in the whole time since he'd joined the Justice Department. Renjiro struggled until he finally managed to discipline his wayward emotions.

He kept up his hard-won facade of control until he made the safety of the ablution units. He couldn't break down, but the fear that speared him, that he might find her again just to lose her... He latched the stall door and levered himself to the seat, his head in his hands. "Gods above." He couldn't stop the groan that escaped.

The years rolled away and once more he remembered the concern in her eyes, the careful way she'd attended him. The light brush of her lips against his. The touches that had been almost incendiary. His body betrayed him, his groin instantly stiffening, and he breathed hard as he tried to clear the latent desire that still lanced him. *It was five years ago*, his mind interjected. *It was only yesterday*, wailed his heart.

Finally, assured that he had controlled his emotions, he stood and let himself out of the stall. The room was empty, but he took a moment, washed his hands, splashed his face, and gripped the sink with closed eyes.

In some deep recess of his mind, he knew, like himself, she'd waited for this. He'd promised himself when she disappeared that he'd find her again. He'd checked every listing of those forcibly removed from Federation space. But he'd never seen her again.

Now, he could and would see her again. He left the ablution block and headed for the Brig. The one where she waited.

Chapter 2

The cell was gray and miserable. Just like the last one she'd seen the inside of, at the conclusion of the war's end celebrations. Selina shivered as a chill invaded her bones. They'd taken her jacket, utility belt, and holster. Standard practice they'd said. It wasn't much help to her as her body temperature dropped.

She currently shared the small cubicle with three other women. Two were drunk and snoring off their inebriation. The third...well, it was clear what her occupation was. The heeled boots ended above the knee and the tight ship suit molded where it touched her body. And a very well endowed body it was too.

The cosmetics she wore were bright. Loud. Crass in shocking purple, green, and black. Her red hair obviously attributed to a bottle.

Selina hugged the corner as the woman yapped at her about how much money she should be out there making. How it was an easy life, if you ignored the odd proclivities of some of the aliens registered on the base, she added with a wink.

Selina's face and knuckles ached like the very devil. Her hands were swollen from the fight, and she was sure the man had torn out chunks of her hair. But she didn't say a word. She knew the routine. Keep calm and hope like hell she could stay under the radar. Maybe they would take pity on her. Give her a warning. So she folded her arms atop her bent knees, propped her head on them like a pillow, and waited.

A sound erupted, shrill as it cut the air. "Oh, see? I'm being bailed already!" The prostitute across the room crowed, and Selina just kept her eyes closed, willing the woman to leave quickly and let her be in silence.

The door opened with a *whoosh* and another chill enveloped her. She shuddered in reaction. The steady march of boots signaled that one of the guards had entered the secured area. "Captain Codecko?"

"Oh, I could be if you want. Hmm, what a big strong boy you are." The woman prattled away as Selina carefully unfolded herself and looked up into a pair of brown eyes she remembered from a long time ago.

"That's me." She stood, unsteadily.

The door clattered open. "Follow me."

Not for the first time, she damned her bad luck. First she'd been on the wrong side of the war, then she'd fallen in with Ashford's plans. Now this. For some reason, the deities seemed to conspire against her.

So she followed the man out of the cell to the ringing endorsements of the prostitute, through the large, triple-sheeted security door, and into a tiny office beyond the charging desk.

"Sit down." His terse words filled her with pain and sadness.

She acceded to his request in silence, holding her

throbbing hand against her breast. He squatted before her, his face close to hers, his dark eyes shadowed. His touch was gentle as his fingers traced the line of her jaw. They shook a little and she felt the glancing caress. It warmed her.

He touched a raw spot on her chin and she hissed involuntarily. "Where else are you injured?"

Selina shook her head.

"Captain Codecko? Selina?"

His gentle words nearly undid her. Tears burned in her eyes and she blinked, hoping to banish them. It didn't work though. They dripped down her face, scalding her frozen cheeks.

Now his hands dropped to her shoulders. "Where else are you hurt, Selina?" His gaze was hypnotic. It drew her words without thought.

"My hand, ribs, and the top of my head."

He frowned and started tugging at her shirt, pulling it free of the loose-fitting pants. "What... What are you doing?"

He glanced at her, his face taut and strained. "I'm checking your injuries."

Selina blushed, the heat creeping over her face as she pushed at his hands. "No! You can't do that!"

"Just bloody watch me." His rough words surprised her and her hands dropped away. He continued his almost feverish work at her buttons and very quickly he had the shirt open. Selina thanked whatever had made her fasten a bra over her very tiny breasts. With gentle movements, he brushed the old material of her shirt to one side. He hissed through clenched teeth at what he saw. "You need a medic."

"I'm fine. I've lived through this before. Of greater

concern to me is whether I'm going to be charged for causing the riot. I was just—"

"I know. Having a quiet drink. We checked the spy eyes. You will be free to go, so long as we can put together a suitable argument. But I have a proposition. One that would help you, I think."

In her experience, propositions never ended well, but she was desperate enough to listen to what he had to say. So she watched in mute silence as he rose. He backed away as she quickly refastened her shirt. Then he paced to the end of the room and back.

"I've just received a communiqué that there's some Indies about to plan an attack on this moon base. I need people I can trust to get information for me."

She waited. But as he started pacing again, it seemed she would need to ask the question. "What's in it for me?"

He stilled.

Selina held her breath. Waiting.

"I might be able to swing an official citizenship for you."

Just like that, he could brush away all the difficulties she had faced since the end of the war. But trusting people didn't come easily. Not for her. "You can just click your fingers and make that happen?"

He faced her again. His eyes shone almost feverishly bright under the lighting of the room. "No. But I know someone who might be able to make it happen, if you agree."

"Why? Why would you help me?"

He smiled. "Because I owe you." The minute Renjiro said the words, he wanted to call them back. Her face shuttered and he wanted to grab her. But they'd only had four days five years ago. Not long enough for her to know that he used flippancy when flustered.

He rose and headed for the door. She didn't follow and that concerned him. The Selina he remembered would have lunged in an attempt to escape.

He jerked the door open and sauntered to the charge desk. The clerk looked at him, expectance clear in her features.

"Can I help you, sir?"

He nodded. "I need you to release the prisoner into my care."

She blinked. "I'm sorry? I don't understand. Are you planning on transferring her to another holding cell?"

"No. Release her into my care. I'll take responsibility for her."

"But sir, the rules state..." She looked shocked, her face leaching to white except for the streaks of cosmetics on her skin.

He knew his actions skirted close to misconduct. "I know the rules. Release her into my care." He leaned forward. "I have my reasons. You don't need to know them."

She nodded furiously and set her fingers to the keyboard. Within minutes he held a leather jacket, holster, utility belt, and the papers he required.

He strode back into the room and stopped, astonished at the sight in front of him. Selina had curled up in the corner and gone to sleep, her head pillowed on her arms. An emotion, deep and rich, flowed through him. *I can't give her up this time.*

In his mind, he'd formulated a plan. One that occurred to him during the time he'd left the ablution block to when he'd received the communiqué. He hadn't been telling her anything untrue. His cousin was a highly placed senator of their homeworld, Reunion, and he might be able to arrange for her to receive citizenship as a reward for services offered to the Federation.

But right now, he needed to get her up and on the way to his apartment on level three. He grabbed the pink tag and replaced it with a deep blue one then roused her, taking care not to hurt her. "Selina? You need to wake up."

"I just want to sleep." Her voice was groggy, and Renjiro frowned once more. Was this exhaustion or something related to her injuries? That concerned him more than he cared to consider.

"Selina, you have to wake up."

She did slowly, her green-brown eyes shadowed, the iris almost totally obscured, and he cursed. "Stand up."

"Where am I?" she whispered, and he noted the lack of color on her face, the slow way she responded. She no longer shivered. Her lips carried a slightly purple-blue tinge. He handed over her jacket and she looked at it before glancing back at him.

"Do I need that?"

Instead of answering, Ren bundled it on her, and she flinched away from his touch for an instant.

"Let's get out of here."

He slid a hand around her waist , and with a sigh, she accepted his touch.

"Where are we going?"

"My apartment. It's on level three."

She stopped, immovable. "But I'm not allowed there."

Selina sounded like a confused child, and he wanted to just lift her into his arms and stride manfully out of the facility, but he couldn't. Instead he spoke slowly, so she'd understand. "You can with me. You have a new tag. A blue tag. It means you're in my care."

"But..."

"Not now, Selina. Just accept what I'm saying." With that, he hustled her out onto the concourse and toward the lifts.

The base was settling in for the night, only shift workers strolled and none paid him any attention as he hustled the woman forward. They entered the lift and he pressed the button for level three, waiting as they dropped down, watching the passing girders and doors until the level he wanted was before them. He hurried her out and down the long hall to his apartment.

The automatic door opened and he tugged her inside.

"So now I'm here, what do you want?" She shrugged off the jacket with a hiss and he looked at her closely, noting the bluish tint on her lips had gone, instead she now had a cunning look on her face. Her fingers found the buttons of her shirt and she threaded the first one through the hole before moving to the second.

"What are you..." The thought fled as inches of pearly skin were uncovered before his startled gaze.

Finally, as the final button gave, she tugged the material from her arms and let it fall from her body. "Where's the bed then?"

She shook, this time not because of cold or because her body ached. Oh no! This was the man of her dreams. The one she had wanted for five long years. The one she'd hidden and nursed then run away from. The one whose name she'd tried to forget. *Renjiro.*

But her body remembered him. Remembered their furtive caresses. The way he'd kissed her, caressed her bared flesh. Not that they'd gone all the way. Every brief and carefully stolen touch had been dangerous, but they hadn't been able to help themselves. She accepted when he left that it was how it had to be, knowing that there was no future.

But after five long years, here he was. Now, abstaining no longer seemed an option as her body clamored.

He stood there, watching her as she'd divested herself of her jacket and shirt. The shock evident on his face would have been funny if she wasn't so sure that this might be their only opportunity for the most intimate act of all. Once he realized there was no way the Federation would allow her citizenship...well, she fully expected to be off on the first repatriation ship they could lay their hands on.

Selina's body ached unmercifully, but she continued her striptease in front of him. The button and zipper of the pants were more of an issue with her swollen hand, but she managed, and the fabric pooled around her heavy black boots.

"Selina, wait!" Renjiro's voice sounded rusty, as if from disuse. But she knew that wasn't true.

"Aren't you planning on getting naked?"

The look he sent her would have been deadly if she hadn't known exactly what he wanted. It was clear, there, in the way he watched her. Hunger. He was definitely hungry if the bulge she detected was anything to go by.

"Don't..."

She leaned forward, stripping away the light bra and hooked her fingers under her panties. With care, Selina pushed away the material, unfastened her boots, and, one by one, dropped them to the ground, and stepped out of her clothes.

"This isn't what I planned."

Selina stopped at the pain in his voice. "I know. But it's been five years, Renjiro. Five long , empty years. I don't want to miss this again." She watched him, the way he swallowed and his Adam's apple bobbed. "I want to feel you touch me. I want you to fill me. I want a memory to ..."

He frowned. "What do you mean? A memory?"

Exasperation colored her words. "You don't seriously think I'll be given citizenship, do you? I mean, I'm an Indy captain. I was the enemy."

He moved forward, his fluid gait unsteady. "Selina..."

"No, Renjiro. Please, give me tonight. If I am given citizenship, it's nothing that will bind us. If they don't..." She swallowed. "Then I'll have a memory to warm me for the rest of my life."

Pain filled his features. "Selina..."

"Please, don't make this hard." Then she laughed at her words. *Hard.* He was obviously that already. "Take me to bed, Renjiro. Please."

Just like that, he moved. A whirlwind of action as he tore at his uniform, jacket flying through the air. His shirt hit the floor with an audible ping and the communicator rolled along the floor. He pulled her against his warm, firm flesh.

She sighed as she felt him against her naked body. "Get the rest off so we can…"

He laughed, the rumble in his chest tickling her nipples, and she caught her breath. Her body was tight, coiled, and ready. Warm. Wet.

She widened her stance, knowing instinctively that he could nestle against the juncture of her thighs, their heights similar. Both were tall, in the region of six feet. That was where the similarities ended. Where she was light skinned with streaked blonde hair, he was bronze with black hair and almond-shaped eyes. He was muscular and she was slight.

His arms wound around her, holding her firmly against him, as his pants dropped to the floor. Now she felt him. All of him. Every glorious inch.

"I've dreamed of you," he muttered unsteadily as he nibbled at her neck. She arched into his caress as his clever fingers skated and touched her. Here and there tiny fires licked at her body. "Every night. And I looked for you."

"Renjiro!" She cried out, unable to string together a coherent sentence. Her body afire with need already. "Fill me, Renjiro! Now."

"Not yet. I need to touch you. To know this isn't some dream. A figment of my imagination." He lifted her with care and strode through the apartment, toeing off his boots as he went. The door to his bedroom opened automatically. She'd never before been so thankful for the remote systems in most apartments.

He laid her upon a bed, dark blue; not much else impinged on her feverishly needy body and mind. He followed her down to the soft surface, then stretched out beside her. She twined one of her legs around one of his and he hissed at the touch of skin against skin.

Her fingers skimmed over his hard musculature before he stilled her. "Let me love you, Selina. The way I have dreamed of for five long years."

She swallowed the instinctive denial as he reached out. His finger lightly touched her breast and circled the areola. It was her turn to burn and shiver. Selina moved, a fluid undulation as the fire stroked her from the inside out.

Then he repeated the action with the other breast. With infinite care, he pulled his hand away and replaced it with his lips. He suckled gently as his hand quested its way down her body, finding the secret dips and valleys and the small strip of hair that hid her secrets.

Renjiro touched her. Gently. Reverently. She bowed up off the covers as her body demanded satisfaction. Tears leaked from her eyes at the tenderness of his strokes. *Five years.* Five years she'd waited for him. Now here they were, together. Just as in her dream.

Her fingers curled around one large bicep, feeling the spot where one of the bullets had entered his flesh. He devoured her now, his lips settled against her own, seeking entry. Their tongues tangled deeply in the cavern of her mouth as their movements became urgent. She pulled away from his kiss as he slid two fingers within her tight wet sheath.

"Fill me, Renjiro. I need all of you." She cried out, and he moved to his knees before withdrawing his hands. Gentle movements parted her thighs then he was between her legs, nudging into position. One slow movement and he slid home. Then he stilled. Her body turned molten.

She swallowed the moan that built within her. The sensation of fullness nearly drove her to a screaming orgasm. Selina gritted her teeth and moved with him. But five years of abstinence on her part was too much and she felt the roll begin deep within. She knew the instant he did too.

His thrusts sped up and the slapping sound of flesh against flesh was loud. It felt like forever as she crested the spike of pleasure, felt him reach the peak just behind her , and cried out as he filled her with one last tremendous thrust.

The moment stopped. With crystal clarity, she knew she'd never feel this emotion with another man, this need for fulfillment. She closed her eyes.

No other man could bring her this. Just Renjiro. And likely, just for one night.

Renjiro lay on his back, listening to Selina's even breathing. Her naked body was nestled tight against his side.

With great care, he reached for the tiny bedside communications unit and dialed his cousin, Reunion's senior senator, on his private unit. Not only was he the senator, he was also the nominal head of the security services division. If anyone could make his proposition work, it was Tomi.

"Tomi here." The voice was groggy, as if he'd been asleep. Renjiro checked the time and cursed. Three AM on Reunion.

"Tomi? It's Renjiro. I need your help." He poured out the situation, leaving nothing, except their now personal relationship, out. He did share that she was there in his apartment with him.

"Tomi, I need her in on the investigation. She's the

only entry I have into the Indy world. She can move where I can't." His stomach roiled and tossed at the idea of using her, but he'd been a soldier far longer than a lover. He knew every advantage had to be utilized. Even if it meant putting Selina in a position he would have avoided if he could. "But in response, I want a citizenship for her."

"Ahh, Renjiro. It's not that simple. We need to know more." The silence grew between them.

Ren counted to ten in his mind before he continued. "Tomi, please." The pleading in his voice was clear. He blushed, but continued. "I need citizenship for her."

"Why?" His cousin's words stopped him in his tracks.

"Because..." A lump formed in his throat as he hunted through his scattered emotions. The truth was stark. "Because I love her, Tomi. I can't let her go. Not this time. I've searched for five years to find her again."

"Ah, Ren. Man. Are you sure?" Ren heard the concern in Tomi's voice.

"Yeah. I'm more sure than I have been of anything else in my life."

"Frick."

He laughed at Tomi's epithet. "That's not really helping, you know."

Selina snuffled in her sleep. He sighed deeply, feeling peace and hope trickle through him. The woman he loved was there, in his bed, beside him.

"Okay then, Ren. Leave it with me. I'll get back to you tomorrow. Meanwhile, take a day off. Don't let her out of your apartment. I'm sure you can think of something to keep her occupied." The last words were said with a dry tone .

"Will do, Tomi. And thank you." His fingers ached and

he realized he'd been gripping the communicator so tightly that his knuckles had turned white.

"Don't thank me yet, cousin. I'll see what I can do."

The connection broke and Renjiro replaced the communicator on its pad.

He stared at the ceiling, hoping Tomi could help them both. They would need more than divine intervention from any deity if they were to save her from the threat of forcible removal from the Federation.

"Renjiro?" Her groggy voice broke through his introspection.

"Hey. Feeling any better?"

"Yeah. But where's the bathroom?"

He snickered loudly. "I'll show you, love."

She stilled at his words. "What did you call me?"

He stopped, the smile dropping away from his face. "Love. I called you love, because I do. I love you."

Her face blanched again, and for a moment he thought she would faint. "Well, isn't that fricking wonderful? 'Cause I love you too, and we don't even know if we can stay together." Her eyes shone as tears welled. He felt the hollowness in his chest again. She blinked furiously in front of him.

"I'll do everything I can."

"Yes, but it might not be enough, Renjiro. Then I'll have to leave. And this time it will hurt more, because I know you feel the same."

"As my grandmother used to say, let's not borrow trouble. Now the bathroom is through here. I'll go get us a drink, and when you're done, come through to me."

Uncaring of his nudity, he padded to the kitchen. The small communicator was on the floor where it had bounced during his energetic striptease. He picked it up and depressed het button.

"Sir?"

"Lola, I won't be in tomorrow. Anything that's urgent, give to Jordan. I'm not to be disturbed."

"Yes, sir." Given his position, it wasn't unusual for him to work with the government privately, so his communication shouldn't raise any eyebrows. At least, not until Jordan realized he had Selina with him. Then there'd likely be trouble.

He was placing the communicator down on the bench as Selina entered the room. She too was naked, and he ran a thoughtful eye over her body. The bruising had settled into a mottled orange after he'd applied a treatment post sex and the bone unit was working on repairing the damage sustained in the fight.

"Would you like a wine?"

She smiled. "That's how this all started, you know. I was in the bar having a Deluvian wine when the fool on my left turned. He was so inebriated that he knocked me into the guy on the other side. I spilled my wine."

He nodded thoughtfully. "That's what we thought." He opened an Earth wine, one that he'd had for a long time. It was a vintage, with grapes actually grown in soil rather than hydroponically. The aroma filled the air, rich and heady. "Try this."

She accepted the glass and sipped cautiously. "Oh my gods! Where on earth did you get this?"

"Right on the first guess." She looked at him blankly.

"On Earth. It's been grown in soil."

Her lips formed a round O and he smiled.

With a careful move, he held out a hand. "Now come to bed with me." He tugged and was rewarded with a blinding smile and her cautious steps. As they entered the bedroom, he retrieved the glass from her hands and set it carefully on the bedside table.

She watched his movements, and he stepped back before he swept her into his arms and set his mouth to hers. She tasted of wine and delectable woman. He was ready to feast again.

Chapter 3

Morning came quickly. Selina stretched out her hands, touching warm flesh. She stilled, and her breath caught. Maybe the dream of last night wasn't a dream after all. She turned, seeing the expanse of firm, bronzed male flesh.

Dark hair shorn over his scalp was a beacon against the crisp, white linen pillows. Unable to stop her action, she reached out, and with a single fingertip touched the springy silk.

Renjiro turned. "Good morning." When his arms folded around her, her breath fled. Their lips touched and the kiss deepened. Took on a life of its own, so deep and rich.

Powerful enough that Selina was sure he was stealing her soul and making it his. Eventually he pulled away and they both panted heavily. "Now that has to be the best way to say good morning that I've ever heard of."

The comm on the bedside gave an imperious noise and reality crashed back down around her.

With his fingers to his lips, he raised the tiny unit and depressed the button. "Renjiro."

"It's Tomi. I've managed a temporary stay while I work on the powers that be. Ren, there's something mighty strange about her files."

Selina stilled, her smile dying away as fear bloomed. She'd never told anyone what Renjiro was about to find out. Not that she'd done anything wrong, just that the truth was far too dangerous. Not just to her, but to the others as well.

If he found out...well, he'd think she'd turned traitor on her own people or something. No one trusted or wanted spies. Least of all someone in Renjiro's position.

"What?" His eyes flicked to hers, and she wanted to tell this Tomi to stop. Not to tell Renjiro. But it was too late. He deserved to know the truth. He needed to know exactly who she was. What the truth she was running from was.

"Ren. She was a spy."

She saw the way he tensed. The hard muscles locking. "What?" He turned, his gaze burning her to the core and she felt empty. Lost.

All she could do now was run. Hope she could elude him. Get away before he learned anything else.

She moved, fast as lightning, out of the bed and into the lounge, grabbing her scattered clothes and tossing them over her body. After this, Renjiro would hate her. Selina couldn't bear to see that in his eyes. He was listening to what Tomi had to say and watching her at the same time. Tomi's voice reverberated through the device, tinny through the tiny speaker, but she refused to stay and listen anymore. With a quick move, Selina snapped up the lanyard with the blue tag and let herself out of the apartment as fast as possible.

The tears were flowing freely as she hurried down the corridor and punched the call button on the elevator. It arrived quickly and Selina tapped her fingers by her side as she waited for the seventh level. As she stepped out, the override light glowed. Time was now precious. He was coming and she had to move. *Move faster!*

She scurried to the berth where the ship lay. No one accosted or stopped her, though many watched her reckless flight. Renjiro hadn't called for any backup—at least not yet— otherwise they'd be here. She was banking on that now. It might be her only salvation.

The men clustered about. "Hey, lady! Captain! The ship is stocked and your cargo arrived almost as soon as you left."

She didn't stop her fast steps. Instead, she redoubled her efforts, pounding up the ramp. "Great. Then I'm out of here."

They gaped at her appearance. No doubt her eyes were rimmed with red and tears trailed down her face. She hurried into the ship and set the locks on the units, retracted the short ramp, and threw herself into her command chair. *No time to waste now. If he knows, he'll let me go.*

She powered up and set the lock release toggle while she disengaged the brakes. The large bay doors started to open, inching slowly as she cast another frightened gaze toward the safe zone.

"*Sylvie's Dream*! You do not have permission to leave the bay. Power down immediately." The voice in the tinny unit was strident. She ignored it as her pain gnawed.

"Sorry, but I'm not waiting." As soon as the clamps released, she engaged the thrusters just enough to pull her away. Now she focused on looking ahead. She refused to look back, to see the cargo bay doors closing. How could she? She was leaving her heart, and yes, her soul, behind on the moon base. With him. *Renjiro!* She ignored the call of her heart.

"*Sylvie's Dream*, power down immediately. You do not have permission to leave this base."

She smiled, but was sure it was bittersweet. She was about to commit the ultimate pilot's sin. "Right now I don't care much. I just have to get out of here."

This time, she gave the thrusters full power in the hopes that she could build up speed, but her thought processes were sluggish and impaired. A lumbering freighter, an old Midgeon Dash Five, cut across her path and she sucked deeply on the oxygen. It was only after she turned the small craft on its side and whizzed past that she drew a full lung-filling breath.

Gods damn it! That was too close. Ashford would have more than just her hide. That is, if Ashford didn't throw her ass out of the chair she was currently filling.

The blackness of stars lay ahead and she made a correction in her head when a *thunk* told her that the escape had been pointless. " *Sylvie's Dream*, power down immediately. This is the Federation vessel *Emancipation*. We are taking you under tow. Our men will board you, and you will submit to our orders or come under fire."

The voice this time was terse. To the point. It was another voice that she knew. She blinked away, but for all they burned, there were no more tears. *I can't even get a gods damned escape right!*

She was defeated before she could run. With a shaking hand, Selina depressed the communications button. "This is the *Sylvie's Dream*. Powering down now." The clank was loud and the ship shuddered. Then came the motion of being pulled backward. Back toward the *Emancipation*.

She let her mind wander, remembering her brief time with Renjiro, five years ago.

The sound of an engine in distress whined above her. She glanced around, but no one was looking. As she always did, she stepped back into the shadows. Let them melt around her. No one had missed her. She turned and ran for the jungle.

She might be able to get information out again. She usually took every possible opportunity to feed the intelligence she'd collected back to the Federation base.

The ship descended slowly. The sound of it touching down surprised her and she waited, hiding in the scrub. Watching to see what would happen next. She was an experienced pilot and knew whoever flew this craft wasn't.

When he emerged, large and imposing, she knew he'd been injured. Men rushed him, but he cast them off, a shot here and a quick lethal move there. Finally he wavered. She could see he was ground forces even as he slumped to the ground.

No one knew either one of them was there. She'd need to act fast.

That had started the long days they'd spent together. The first day, he'd been delirious , but she'd stayed, nursed him, and ensured his craft was hidden.

By the second day, he'd opened his eyes. And she'd been lost. The sense of belonging had overtaken her. Growing up in an orphanage, it wasn't an emotion she had a lot of experience with. By the third day's end, they'd kissed and caressed and she'd lost her heart to this man.

When she fled on the fourth day, his name was emblazoned on her heart.

Renjiro's chest hurt. She'd run from him. *Why?* Once Tomi explained the situation, it made no sense. She'd been working for the Federation before being left to fend for herself. She'd been their spy. They'd done the wrong thing by her, then some drone had covered it up. Left her with no safety net when she needed it most. The jumbled thoughts confused him.

So why did she run?

He'd cut Tomi off and hurried after her, but he'd been too late. On every front. The ship bay was empty, the great metal doors closed. And no ship was present.

The crew who had restocked the supplies stood around, watching the comings and goings with interest.

"You after the captain? She left. Looked pretty upset to us." They all nodded and the knot in his belly had doubled in size.

The helplessness that assailed him got bigger when he saw Jordan, his second-in-command, was making his way up the corridor. He'd been red faced and furious. "With all due respect, sir... What the hell happened?"

Even though he trusted Jordan, he couldn't break Tomi's confidence. Even if he had wanted to, there was no way he was going to do that right there. "Jordan, I can't tell you."

His second's mouth thinned into a long white line. "That's not good enough. We stuck our neck out for you and then she..." He stopped, blinked , and shook his head. "Sir...Commander Ito, we have to report this to the Traffic Control and the Moon Base Governor. Then on top of that, we have the military—"

"Who will only deal with me. Jordan, this is one case where you don't need to know." The man blushed deeper.

Renjiro knew it was simply a case of being unable to accept the blanket ruling, but in this instance, even though it looked bad, there was nothing he could do. His hands were effectively tied.

"Sir, I must protest."

"It is noted. Jordan, there is more than meets the eye. Just trust me."

The man searched his face and gave a begrudging nod. "I'd like my protest noted formally."

Renjiro nodded. "Do so. Then return to my office. I will be out all day."

Even as Jordan backed away, Renjiro noted the communication device buzzing. "Yes?"

"Commander, this is Governor Ingra. Please tell me why a vessel carrying an Indy under a blue tag registered to you failed to respond to Traffic Control."

"Governor, at this time I cannot give you that information. As soon as I am at liberty, I will share what I can." Weariness threaded through his voice. He'd been awake less than an hour and he already felt as if he'd completed a grueling day of training.

"This is a government matter?" The voice was steady and probing.

"It is." There was silence and the comm badge now winked blue, another call. "Governor, I have another incoming I must take. If you will permit me?"

"Indeed, Commander. But I will expect a full briefing as soon as you can." Then the connection died.

"Yes?"

"Commander Ito, this is Captain Carmichael Snow. I am requesting your presence aboard the *Emancipation*. I need to have a discussion with you, I believe."

Carmichael Snow was a legend in military circles with

his impressive military record. Why would the captain of the *Emancipation* be requesting his presence? His thoughts were firmly on where the hell Selina had gone to and he wasn't sure he could cope with further intrigues right now.

Renjiro wanted to scream and yell. To kick the walls. Anything to wash off the frustration building inside himself. "Of course, Captain."

"I'll send my personal skip over to pick you up. And Commander? You might not wish to discuss this visit."

The layer of secrets would normally whet his appetite, but his concern for Selina over rode everything. "I understand."

He moved at a rapid clip, heading for the berth such skips used. He arrived in time to see the tiny craft land. As he stepped on board, the men closed the hatch and indicated he should take a seat. The trip was quick and uneventful. The *Emancipation* was reached in a matter of minutes. The crew members escorted him to a room several decks above the hangar bay. As the door opened, he reared back in surprise. There, in a seat, waiting for him was Selina and the larger-than-life Captain Carmichael Snow.

"So glad you could make it, Commander. Take a seat. I think we have some things to sort out."

Confusion and not a little anger filled him. *What is Selina doing here?* "Selina?"

She shook her head, looking shell-shocked and pale. "Renjiro, if only you hadn't found out. I never meant to lie to you. I just couldn't..."

"It's okay Selina. I..." He cast a glance at Captain Snow who was watching, obviously fascinated by their interaction. "We can discuss this later." But he reached out and gripped her hand to let her know he wasn't angry. It wasn't nearly enough, but for now it would have to do.

"So, now that we're all here, I'm confused about what has happened to my good friend, Selina. To be honest, she served the Federation faithfully. So why has she been stripped of citizenship?"

He lowered himself into the chair, but Renjiro had the impression of fury which belied his soft words and determined cool demeanor.

"I don't know. Selina?"

She averted her gaze and anger welled inside him. Something had happened. But what? He needed her to trust him if they were to fix what had happened. *If they could,* whispered his mind.

"Selina, when you left my compound, you were promised indemnity after you were finished. What the hell happened?"

She hung her head and mumbled.

"Damn it, Selina. I can't hear you!" Renjiro raised his voice before he dropped himself back into the seat, frustrated at his misdirected anger. *What the hell am I thinking, yelling at her?*

"Settle down, Ito. Yelling at Selina won't help anything."

Huddled in the chair, Selina felt a mixture of anger, hurt, and frustration warring deep inside her. It wasn't her fault that their CO had left them all swinging. Damn it, she was just trying to make the best of the bad lot dealt her.

"He refused our paperwork. Made out we'd forged it. He went up the ladder. We went out the door as liars and thieves."

Carmichael stopped her. "What? Who?"

Renjiro's eyes narrowed and his face turned to granite.

"The commander in charge of our division. Winstead. We were warned never to make contact with you or... Otherwise he'd..." She broke off, knowing she was about to commit what to Winstead was the cardinal sin. She was about to tell it all. No doubt, it was also the signing of her own death warrant.

"He'd what?" Renjiro's voice held a dangerous edge, one that she'd never heard from him before.

She shuddered. *How on earth can I tell him?* But the implacable look on his face was chilling.

"Selina?"

The words nudged her. She shook her head then realized Winstead would think she told anyway. There was no benefit in not telling now. "He'd find us. Hunt us down like dogs and put us out of our and his misery." She whispered the words, knowing that would fuel his barely restrained rage. Carmichael was a cold, driven man when his ire was up. But Renjiro? She had the feeling he was capable of more than she'd ever seen.

When they'd met before, he'd been a soldier. Highly decorated and capable. He'd single-handedly taken out five operatives in close hand-to-hand combat after being injured. But that was five years ago. She wasn't sure what more he was capable of. Only that he'd bulked up more, and his eyes carried a cold distance that frightened her.

"I'll find him. Crush the bastard," Renjiro muttered, and she glanced at him, startled by the fury she saw dancing in his eyes.

"But, Renjiro—"

"No, Selina. I..." He stopped, looked at Carmichael. "I need to talk to Selina alone."

Carmichael quirked an interested brow. "Is that so? Then why was she fleeing the moon base?"

Renjiro blushed scarlet, but remained silent, and she felt anger at Carmichael for his comment. At his challenging attitude.

"Carmichael, it's hardly your business." She strained forward, hoping to stress the point. But he ignored it.

"Of course it is. When one of my prize students is treated like this, then feels she has to flee? Let's just say I take a great interest in what happens to you, when I have the opportunity."

"It's personal. Between us."

Carmichael just grinned at her words though. "It might be, but Traffic Control requested our assistance. That makes it my business."

She wanted to lunge across the table and beat him for the frustration he was causing. She glanced at Renjiro, who sat beside her. He radiated a level of anger that flowed off him in palpable waves.

"My cousin is Senator Tomi Ito. He shared certain information—classified information— with me. It caused a misunderstanding between us." Renjiro sat straight and proud in his chair, though the lingering crest of red washed his cheeks.

"So you knew about Selina?" Carmichael leaned forward now, his beefy arms resting on the desktop. His blue eyes blazing.

Renjiro silently inclined his head to inspect Carmichael. "Everything?"

Renjiro looked at Carmichael for a long pregnant

moment before shaking his head. "No. Tomi didn't have access to everything. But she ran before I could talk to her, before I could explain my reaction. Tomi wasn't aware until yesterday that I'd been looking for Selina for five years. We'd met on Seicha Two Seven Seven, when she saved me."

Carmichael's mouth dropped open, and he swiveled in her direction. "Frick! What the hell were you doing there?"

She smiled at Carmichael's demand. "Running pilots mainly. Gathering data. Intelligence. Helping injured comrades." She smiled at Renjiro, unable to stop herself.

He grinned back. It filled her with warmth. Something she'd been sadly lacking since this whole mess erupted.

"Then why did you run?" Her smile melted away at Renjiro's words.

How to explain? "I'm... I was a spy. I fought on the other side, haphazardly, but enough that they believed me to be what I said. I killed those on our side to make my way in. Knowing that, knowing everything I did... How could you want me?" Saying the words out loud hurt. She didn't want to look at his face, but the need to know, once and for all, now, burned.

"How could you..." He stopped, his words dripping with hurt. "You think so little of me? You think I'm so shallow that..."

In that instant the truth blasted through her. She was wrong. He knew why and understood.

"Oh gods, Renjiro. It never occurred to me. I didn't understand because I've always been on my own. I never thought anyone would want me."

He rose with a jerk to take those last few steps, before lowering himself down and wrapping his arms around her.

"Never again. Never will you be alone again. You, Selina. You are the family I choose."

45

Chapter 4

Renjiro stood. He'd known Carmichael was watching, but didn't care. Selina needed him. Needed the reassurance only he could give. With his arms wrapped tightly around her, he fancied she drew the strength she needed.

Carmichael coughed and Ren couldn't help but smile at the captain's discomfort. The link between he and Selina was firmer than ever. They could build a solid base of love and support now that they both knew where the other was coming from. He knew he'd do anything to protect Selina.

"So. Thankfully, the mushy lovey-dovey stuff is out of the way. What do we do next? Selina can't just automatically receive citizenship, otherwise that will tip off Winstead."

The positive emotion fizzled away like a thief in the night , and he drew back from her. "Renjiro mentioned a proposition," Selina said.

He stilled at her words. Although he knew there was another possible way, he didn't want her involved in the furtive world of spying. He didn't want her anywhere near any kind of possible danger.

Carmichael quirked a brow again and he flushed, feeling the tide of red and the heat on his face. "There's a problem with some disaffected Indy's. Word on the ground is they're planning something to disrupt the current economic situation here. I don't have anyone with the capabilities she has. The contacts. I was going to use that to trade for citizenship for Selina. But..."

"You have some powerful connections if you could pull that off." The man opposite frowned for an instant, and Ren got the impression he was thinking over the various options. "You'd use your political capital to get Selina citizenship and round up those disaffected."

"It's a trade of skills. We would all win that way." Ren knew it was more than that. He'd wanted to use it to keep Selina close by. So he could grow a meaningful relationship with her. Maybe even more. "But surely, once you get Winstead..."

"That will take time."

The words were a blow. Time was something they didn't have. "No. It needs to be done before she is shipped out." Ren's chest tightened with concern.

Carmichael smiled. "I think we can make the other work for us though. Tell me more. What kind of plot?"

Renjiro sat back down, unwilling to involve her. He realized Carmichael wouldn't give him that option. "Indy pilots who've been disaffected. You know how they are. They get angry. They want to fight the system. They don't want to follow any of our rules. Hell, they rarely follow their own these days." He looked over to Selina who sat quietly, listening intently.

"They want to disrupt commerce? Cause what? An

explosion? It would have to be a large freighter or something similar. Something that would shut down the port systems." Her insightful question made him smile with pride.

"That and they want to land a blow on the Federation that took over their worlds. They don't see that wasn't what happened. The Federation welcomed the Indy planets only after they asked for entry. They made the overtures, not us."

Selina nodded again. "You need someone who understands their language. Who is a true independent. Someone who can get them to talk freely. I know exactly who you need on the moon base."

He looked at her, startled. "Who?"

"Well, I've been an Indy for over four years. Since the end of the war. Who else was I going to talk to? Who else was going to tip me off that cargo needed shipping? Ashford wasn't. He wouldn't bestir himself. In fact, the only thing I'm expecting when I get back to *Sylvie's Dream* is my marching orders. He's not exactly an easy man to work with."

Carmichael stood. "Who is your contact on the moon base?"

"My contacts are tenuous, but Jensen Orden. He's a small freighter with links back to the main hierarchy. I kept tabs on all my contacts, because I might have needed them sometime. I didn't exactly have a lot of friends anymore, you know." She spoke in a matter-of-fact way, but he heard the loneliness she couldn't conceal.

Now that he knew it was a simple matter of infiltrating, his mind whirred into action. Surely it wouldn't be too dangerous? It was a wishful thought, he knew, but he clung to it while his mind ran through options, chances, and ways they could make this plan work. But it would mean being separated. That didn't meet with his approval, or hers, he would bet.

"I don't know Orden. When we get back I can look him up." He looked up at her. "But you won't be able to stay with me. You'll need a new pink tag. I'm sorry. If we do this..."

She smiled and squeezed his hand. "No. But that will come. So. What do we do next?"

"We'll need to transfer you back to the moon base. Make it believable. Maybe lock you in the brig for some time then release you back onto the three levels. Of course, that's where Orden would be, so chances are..."

"I'll run into him sooner rather than later. Yes." She nodded, thoughtful. "Well, I guess that's the only way forward. Carmichael, can you arrange for my things to be retrieved from *Sylvie's Dream*?"

He nodded silently and Renjiro understood why. They were all she had. Every little thing would be meaningful to her. "I'll look after them. Get them safely to Ito's. Then I'll arrange your return to the brig. We can let it slip that I found you interesting..."

Selina's look told him his part of the plan had holes large enough to ram a freighter ship through. "No, not unless you make a habit of this kind of behavior. Arrange my passage back, then stick me in another brig. Perhaps the one closest to you. Keep me there for say a day, then release me. It's believable and achievable."

It didn't suit him. She'd be so close and yet so very far away. But he couldn't argue with her logic. As she and Carmichael expanded the plan, he watched them work. She was comfortable and easy in the role. It intrigued and aroused him.

He'd have to ignore that for now.

Once they agreed on the plan, Carmichael lent him restraints, and with a quick apology, he had her cuffed and headed for the small skiff.

They traveled in silence, aware that at any time someone might be listening. It was only when they reached the brig next door to his office that he pulled her aside, into his office. "Stay safe. Remember, I love you and am looking forward to a long future with you."

They embraced quickly then he had Jordan direct her to a cell. It was all he could do to watch her leave.

***

Selina waited in the tiny cell. They'd taken her jacket again and the chill seeped into her bones. Renjiro had apologized quietly while taking it, and she knew he worried. Yet, it was a struggle to keep her face impassive when all she wanted to do was grin.

Carmichael would deal with Winstead, but it had to be stealthy, he'd assured them. Until then, they were to continue dealing with Renjiro's problem. She mulled it over in her mind. How to contact Orden was the biggest sticking point. "Orden, where would you be right now?"

She could contact him by communicator, but that would look odd. In the years following the war, they'd used word of mouth—Indy-to-Indy—to keep track of their peers. Using communicators wasn't safe for those living on the fringes.

No, she needed to casually bump into him. Maybe at one of the bars. He'd always liked to wash off his anger in a tankard or three of ale it what she'd heard was correct. Of course, the sooner *Sylvie's Dream* returned to dock, the more believable it would keep the tale she needed to tell.

Renjiro had assured her he'd make sure she was back in the original dock. As soon as they sprang her, she would make her way back there. To the ship that had been home for the last several years, since she'd teamed up with Ashford. It was another step. No doubt she'd be locked out, but she needed to try. Needed to say goodbye.

Seeing the ship, but likely not being able to board it was sure to be a wrench. She'd enjoyed piloting the old bird, but the time had come to move on, and she had the hope of a bright future now.

A rattle and clank heralded the arrival of the guard. She caught sight of the blond hair and stormy features. *Jordan.* Damn, Ren had deputized him to deal with her. She'd seen his acid look earlier when he'd taken her from Renjiro's office. He was clearly upset that she'd duped Renjiro. Or so he thought. She wondered what he'd told Jordan, but refused to ask.

"Get up. You're free to go."

"Free? Where's my jacket?"

He ignored her, just gestured for her to move through the doorway. She headed through the opening and out into the charging area. Men and women filled the small room and she waited. She needed her jacket, utility belt, and holster back.

He snatched them up from a desk and thrust them at her. "The sooner you're gone, the better things will be."

She smiled and it took some effort to force her lips into the action. She hoped he'd forgive her eventually, then shrugged off the thought. "Fine, I'm gone."

She set off; long, easy strides took her through the corridor and out onto the concourse. She knew where she was, and the level she was on. Without chancing a look either way, she headed for the lift, thrusting her hand into the pocket of her jacket. The tracker was exactly where Renjiro had told her it would be. She ran her thumb along it, grateful for the small device which now acted as a tangible link to Renjiro.

Once aboard the lift, she determinedly faced forward, watching the girders and metal doors until she reached level seven. The doors whooshed open and she strode down to the berth. It hadn't even been twenty-four hours since she'd last been there, but it felt so surreal to be back at the *Sylvie's Dream*. But unlike last time, no one was there to watch her bid goodbye to the freighter.

"I wonder where everyone is." The muttered phrase echoed. She shrugged and headed up the ramp, taking her time, quite sure that she would be locked out of the primary systems. Ashford was quick at dealing with those who caused him issues.

She tapped her unlock sequence, but the light determinedly glowed red. Just as she'd expected. A message flashed on the screen. *Auto systems denied. Error Emp 01 - Termination of Contract.*

She hissed. "So he's already worked it out." She laid her head against the cold gray metal, her fingers touching the locked door. "Thank you, *Sylvie*. You've been the best ship ever. I hope your next pilot appreciates you as I did."

Selina pulled back. She'd prepared herself for this, but a hollowness existed in the pit of her belly.

This was the only way she had a chance of a future with Renjiro, and not even for *Sylvie's Dream* would she give it up. Instead, she made her way to the concourse, snagging a small directional reader to help her find every possible bar on the moon base. She stopped into the first and bought a cooling drink, sipping it thoughtfully until the bartender came over.

"Umm, I'm looking for Jensen Orden," she said.

The man just shook his head and she looked at the tankard then the back of the retreating barman. *Nothing more to learn here.* She pushed away from the bench and left, heading for the next public house.

She repeated the pattern several times, with no success on the seventh level. On the eighth she visited five bars. Already she could recite her request by rote as the fogginess of the alcohol crept along her senses. "I better not drink any more alcohol."

She entered another bar. This one was dirty, grimy almost, and she didn't want to consider what she might find on the seats. So she stood at the bar, ordered a drink she had no intentions of touching, and asked after Jensen Orden.

"I might. Why you looking for him?"

"I knew him many years ago. I'm looking for work and hoping he might help me out." Excitement zinged through her. Finally! Her hand strayed to her pocket, and she ran her thumb over the small locator button once more.

"Reckon if he wants to meet, he'll choose where and when. Where you staying?"

Selina wrinkled her nose. "I haven't found anywhere yet. No one has a vacancy."

"Hostel next door. Tell them Gravind sent you. They'll find a spot. If Orden wants you, he'll find you there."

Knowing she'd been dismissed, Selina pushed away from the bar. "I'll go now."

The man merely nodded.

Renjiro watched on his palm system as she moved again. The tracker was working efficiently and it gave him some peace, knowing where she was at any point in time. This time she had found her way to a small hostel on the eighth level. He knew it well. It wasn't the best place on the moon base, but while the rooms were basic, they were private, clean, and cheap. It was also favored by prostitutes and freighter crews.

His fingers curled around the unit as a knock came at his door. He slipped t he reader into a drawer as he called out to the person on the other side.

Jordan entered, his eyes stormy. "She's been cast off from the *Sylvie's Dream*. I've just received word from the traffic authority. Her contract was cancelled."

Selina had told him that was what she expected. It took every ounce of willpower not to smile. "Then I suppose she's going to be looking for work. Come on Jordan, why are you so concerned?"

"Because she nearly made a mockery of you and our systems." The man was vibrating with anger and some other undefined emotion.

"Nearly, but she didn't, did she? We got her back and as it turns out, the only thing she was guilty of was—"

Jordan placed both hands on the desk, his knuckles white. "Evading the authorities, causing a snafu in the traffic systems."

"And each of those is nothing more than a petty misdemeanor." Renjiro pushed back into his seat as anger welled. He wanted desperately to tell his second he had no idea of the deep game they were playing.

He stopped himself before he said anything. It was a

covert mission. Even so, the thought that she was being treated as a petty criminal burned him.

"But without a contract, she's ineligible to remain in the Federation." Jordan's eyes gleamed. "Let me find her and authorize her removal, sir. Then we can close the file and no one will know what happened."

The lump in Renjiro's throat was back. *Hell, here's a sticky problem indeed. One I knew would come eventually, just not yet.* "Let's leave it for today. The problem could go away overnight. All we have to do is—"

"But sir, we could—"

"No. Leave it for now, Jordan. That's..." He closed his eyes, about to do something very unlike him. "That's an order."

"Sir?" He knew Jordan didn't understand. There was an emotion which he thought was shock in the single word utterance.

"Jordan, don't. Just leave it alone."

"Yes, sir." Jordan's stiff tone spoke volumes about his level of frustration.

Selina had to follow through and do her bit, and he couldn't afford to jeopardize the plot they'd hatched. She was their only opportunity to find a way in. Once she was in contact with Orden... Well, then it wasn't a huge leap at all. She could find out who was involved. That's all they needed to plant someone firmly in the group.

But he did damn the fact that he couldn't see her. Be with her. He needed to know she was safe. On one level, he was aware that she knew what she was doing, but it didn't make it any easier to accept. His hand curled into a fist. It felt wrong knowing she was doing this, but what other option was there?

He looked up at Jordan, noted the scowl, and sighed

inwardly. "I've paperwork to attend to, so unless there's anything else…"

Jordan bowed in silence and retreated.

Slowly, Renjiro started his computer, found the files he needed to work on, and immersed himself as best he could, but his mind wandered in a skittish fashion.

By thirteen hundred hours he was pacing, waiting for anything that would tell him they were moving forward with their inquiries. So when the communicator beeped, he answered it immediately.

"Renjiro here." His stomach coiled. *Who is it this time?*

"Carmichael. I need to meet you. Eatery on the fifth floor far end. Zone something."

"I know the one. When?" *What has gone wrong?*

"Now."

The single word had him heading through the door like a flash, tugging on his jacket and striding for the lifts.

The rapping on the door took Selina by surprise as she stepped out of the ablution unit. "Just a minute." She threw the towel on the bed and pulled on the uniform she'd discarded. Her holster contained one tiny but lethal laser pistol, and she slipped it into the small of her back, down the pants.

She carefully opened the door, with one hand on the auto stop button.

In front of her was a face she hadn't seen in over five years, even then it had been a fleeting acquaintance. Jensen Orden. He hadn't changed from the squat, hard-faced man of her memories of Seicha. No hair adorned his head. His clothes were a faded blue work overall that sagged in the middle. He looked as grubby and unkempt as she recalled.

"So, I heard you were here looking for me, Codecko."

She stilled her grimace, grabbed her aging leather jacket, and thrust her arms into the long sleeves. "You know me, Orden. I turn up like a bad credit. Look, I have a problem and need some assistance."

He grunted, never really one for much talk. "Not here. I have a place."

She engaged the door and followed him down the narrow gray hall to the exit. "It is far?"

"Nah. Just this way."

Her fingers sought for and found the tiny button. She hoped like hell Renjiro was watching where she was headed. Something about this felt wrong on a lot of levels. She'd always trusted her instincts and right now, they were screaming.

He opened a tiny, nondescript door and she found they were in the middle of a long corridor filled with sheds. They were dirty and battered. He led her to one and she stepped into the dark of the small enclosure. Movement in the corner caught her eye. "Who's here?"

"Codecko. Never thought I'd see you again."

Oh gods no! She knew that voice, and it wasn't one she ever wanted to hear again. *Winstead.*

Renjiro hurried along the concourse, seeing the eatery ahead. He ignored the raucous music and cries of the touts. People brushed past him, but he didn't pay any attention. Waiting outside was the imposing form of Carmichael. He hunched over, as if trying to hide his height, but nothing could disguise the barely leashed power. His eyes narrowed as soon as he spotted Renjiro, and for a heartbeat, Ren was filled with fear.

What would make Carmichael take the chance of meeting him face to face? Why now? Why here?

Carmichael held the door. "We can talk inside. I had my men book the place out."

If he has to take such extreme steps... "Selina?"

"I don't know. Inside." The man gestured to the inside of the eatery and Renjiro nodded. He ducked his head and hoped no one had paid too much attention to his attendance there. It wasn't like him to be out at this time of day. Nor did he want the fast exchange to take place in public. He followed Carmichael in, and his stomach was a mass of coiling and tossing snakes.

Carmichael headed to a table in the far corner, hunkering down, his back against the wall. A classic pose, thought Renjiro. It was the same kind that Selina used.

"We have credible information that Winstead is here, on Moon Base 703. I think he somehow realized she was here too. We have intercepted a communication with some Indy freighters. Renjiro, she could be in danger."

It was a blow, one he physically reeled from. "We have to find her."

Carmichael stared at him. "Yes, we do. But that means someone knows. I haven't told anyone. Who have you told?"

His heart stopped thudding in his chest. When it resumed, it was a sickly and pale shadow of his normal beat. *Jordan.* Only Jordan knew there was more to his actions.

Nausea rose, hot and bitter. "Only my second knows a little. Not a lot. Just that something is going on."

"Thank heavens for small mercies then. But what exactly does he know?" Carmichael leaned forward. "And where is Selina?"

Renjiro pulled out the small handheld device. "Eighth level. A small... A small engineering unit full of sheds near the hostel."

His mind hit overdrive. *What if we're too late?* For an instant he panicked, feeling the force of his concerns crashing down upon him. Then his training kicked in and he calmed himself. Searched for his center to latch onto. Found it, like a drowning swimmer with a lifebelt. He hung on for dear life. Or at least, Selina's. She was a trained spy. He'd seen her in action before. She could take care of herself. Still, the what if's floated through his mind.

"You go find your man. Leave Selina to us."

"No. I can't. Surely you must see..." Even though his brain told him she was safe, he couldn't leave her to Carmichael.

Carmichael smiled. It was a sardonic uptick of his lips. "And what if your man—"

"I can set him a task. Make it so that he's busy." All the while his mind shifted and examined possible options at lightning speed. He tapped his communicator. "Renjiro to Jordan?"

"Jordan here, sir."

"Good. I need you to do something for me. I overlooked the latest claims against overtime. Bella has been pinging me since last week about them. Can you clear them? They're urgent." Silence met his request. Then a sigh.

"Of course. Do you wish me to add you to the report when complete?" He heard the stiffness in Jordan's words and the realization of what Jordan was, hit him. Jordan was the traitor.

"Yes. Renjiro out."

Carmichael pinned him with a glance. "Overtime?"

"It's honestly all I could think of. And it is urgent. Bella, from credit applications, has been requesting them as urgent for the last week. It will keep him in the office and busy. For now, anyway."

The man opposite shrugged. "Whatever works."

They rose, as did the men and women in the eatery. Dozens of eyes were trained on him. "They'll follow you in a variety of different directions. Once they know where."

He gave the directions. Noted the way they split off in groups. Some to follow him to the lifts, others would take transportation from other locations. Some would be more covert in their actions he knew. Renjiro just hoped they made it in time.

Chapter 5

Selina's stomach was quivering. "So, Winstead, what are you doing here?" This was a trap she'd wandered into. One she hadn't even conceived. She'd be willing to bet neither had Renjiro or Carmichael.

Winstead stared at her, his blond hair sticking up in spikes with purple and blue tips that matched his immaculate ship suit, his finger rubbing slowly across his hairless upper lip. "Oh dear, Codecko. Is that any way to greet a long lost friend?" The leer he gave her left ice in her veins. Chilled, she tried to pull away, but Orden had grabbed her arms, forcing them painfully together behind her back, his meaty hands like manacles.

"You were never a friend. But how the hell did you persuade Orden to work with you?" His smile was the signature oily smile she remembered from years ago. Except his face didn't respond quite so easily. He'd no doubt undergone many transformative and re-aging treatments in the last five years, she deduced.

"Oh dear. You do have it so wrong. Orden is an Indy

who I've been allied with for a good many years. Even back during the war he gave me information." The look he gave Selina sickened her.

He stood then moved forward, each step careful. The spiteful gleam in his eyes was of more concern. She knew from past experience he would lash out and strike when least expected, and he did so with glee. She'd been on the receiving end of those nasty jabs in the past. He did so now, delivering a stinging slap across her cheek. The same one that bore the scrapes from the bar room brawl.

"I knew from your report that you'd had contact with Commander Ito previously. Let me see, it was the skirmish on Seicha Two Seven Seven, wasn't it? Yes, I know all about your actions."

He grinned as she blinked back the tears, her face stinging. *How the hell am I going to get out of this mess? And what does he know about me and Renjiro?*

She struggled, pulling against Orden's hold, but he just gripped tighter. Delivering more pain and bruises for her trouble.

"Anyway, I kept tabs on you, and when the information was received from my contacts here... Well, let's just say, I reacquainted myself with your files." He leered, looming close. "I told you not to contact anyone from those times. But you never listened. Not even then."

Crack! Another quick blow split her lip and she contained the cry.

"Now, obviously I don't have a lot of time. My work with the senate has brought me here, surprisingly enough, to undertake discussions with the governor, and I'm expected at a function soon. So I won't make you wait too much longer."

He stepped back and, for the first time, she noted the restraints attached to a girder. "You won't get away with this. Others know. They'll bring you down even if you——"

"Oh, do be quiet, tiresome woman." He picked up an implement, long and thin. He flicked it and it whistled through the air. "I rather like some of the affectations of ancient history. This one in particular is fun. It's called a whip." He used it and it cut through the air.

Meanwhile, Orden gripped her, propelling her backward toward the girder. She inhaled deeply, filling her lungs, and prepared to scream. Just as she opened her mouth, the whip struck across her midsection and she doubled over. Blood seeped over her uniform. The cut wasn't deep, she was sure, but it hurt.

Pain radiated though her entire body. Her breath was short and she panted. Each expansion of her lungs felt like a knife in her solar plexus.

She gasped and Orden gripped her hands, fastening them firmly before pushing her back. Even as she pulled and tugged, he fastened her legs tightly, and she knew they would quickly cut off the circulation.

"Orden, don't do this."

He just grinned, showing a mouth of missing and cracked teeth at her thin request. A rag was thrust in her mouth and a bandage wound around to hold it firm. "Oh, I rather like where I am. Better than where you are."

Orden moved and fear spiked as Winstead took his position in front of her. His arm pulled back and he struck. Once. Twice. A third time. She cried out as pain arced through her, but the sound was muffled by the rags.

"You never were much good at listening. So here's your chance." Now Winstead straightened his jacket and stood straight and tall, his eyes gleaming with delight in the darkness. "We'll be leaving you here. Alone. Maybe before you die, you'll become more adept at listening. No one will hear you. They'll be so close, yet so far away. Ah well, that's how spies die. Quietly. Unseen and unheard."

Then he turned and left the tiny shack, followed by Orden. The lights winked out as tears slid down her face once more. These of frustration and anger, more so than pain.

At least they hadn't stripped her jacket, she thought. Renjiro would still be able to find her with the help of the tracking device. Questions formed in her mind. *Who? Who had told? Who was the person in Renjiro's office?*

Time passed and blurred.

The pain overtook her and for the first time in her life, she fainted.

Renjiro hurried with Carmichael in tow, his heart pounding in his chest as he exerted every bit of energy, pushing out a burst of speed. In his brain came the tattoo of *hurry, hurry.* His mind screamed that speed was of the essence. The fact that he couldn't call in his own people angered him. *A cuckoo in my own nest.* It was insupportable. But he couldn't afford to tip them off. Not yet. The thought nearly unmanned him. For all his lofty position, there was nothing he could do other than what he was doing, and it wasn't nearly enough.

They had reached the eighth level and he moved, knowing exactly where the sheds were, but he couldn't pinpoint exactly which one, as there were rows of them.

He cursed. He might know every inch of this damned moon base from his hours of patrols, but there was no simple fix for determining which one she was in.

He checked the designation of each shed, the dirty green numbering hard to read, covered in dust and the years of neglect. He opened every unlocked door and peered within. The darkness illuminated only by the small light stick he carried. But each bay he checked was empty.

He left those latched to come back to, reasoning that surely she'd be in one... One that was already open. It was a vain hope.

Ren's mind blanked.

He didn't want to consider what he might find and couldn't afford to crack the small modicum of composure he had left.

At the end of the bays he stopped, scratched the back of his head, and cursed. "Nothing. Start checking the locked ones. I'll start this end, you on that."

Carmichael glanced at him, no doubt wondering if he'd lost his mind. Probably he had now, and surely the man could tell, but he accepted the task without a word. He patted his belt, seeking the key chain. No building or room could be locked against him and his officers. They moved as fast as they dared, rattled each door, then used Renjiro's master keys to unfasten the old-fashioned locks. As they checked each they called "Clear," before moving on. Each *clear* was another nail in the coffin of his tenuous hope.

Exhaustion was setting in as the adrenaline seeped out. Each empty shed delivered another blow, sapping his will and strength.

He rested his head for a moment against the next door.

Sweat left a wet halo on the metal and he breathed heavily before he pushed away and attempted the next. He noted the new locks. There were several of them as well as tightly wound chains. His heart lifted again and he shoved the door open, peering inside.

His breath caught.

He must have cried out because Carmichael was there in an instant.

He moved quickly, seeing the way she hung, fastened to the girder, her body limp, and a coppery taint filled the air, overriding the stink of oils and rags.

He heard her shallow breathing and noted the oozing blood that coated her, but gave thanks to every deity as he moved behind her. With shaking hands he found the clasps that held her up and freed her feet before her arms.

She slumped, but Carmichael was there to catch her in his arms.

Renjiro cleared a patch of grimy floor. "Lay her down on the ground so I can check her." By the light of the illuminated stick, he tugged out his medical recorder, checking her for serious injuries first, anything life-threatening. The scans showed bruising and lacerations, but no internal damage or broken bones.

"It's mainly superficial." He bowed his head over her supine figure, digging deep in his emotional well.

She was alive. He could breathe again.

She was injured, but would make a full recovery. Fury hummed and scoured his veins. Heat filled him.

A sound roused him. Selina was coming to. "Ren... Renjiro?" Her words were weak and slurred. He captured her hand.

"I'm here, baby. I'm with you." He squeezed carefully and exulted when she returned the caress.

She smiled, but it was a weak facsimile of her usual grin. "Orden... He's working with Winstead. He's here on the moon base. Meeting with the governor."

Alarm filled him. "Damn, we need to get you out of here and into the care of a medic." She shook her head though and her hair billowed and she hissed, he guessed, with pain.

"No, I need to come with you. Be there when you get him. Renjiro? He knew about us. Possibly Tomi too."

He cursed in all the languages he knew. If Winstead had that information, more than a few could also be in danger. They didn't have time to get her to a medic. If he made it to the governor's private level, they had no ability to take Winstead into custody. It was a zone of diplomatic immunity.

Carmichael was already ordering the men and women who poured toward the shed with new instructions. Most of them took off. While Renjiro really wanted to be there at Winstead's capture, his place right now was here with Selina.

He slid his hands beneath her and lifted her against his chest with great care. "I won't ever let them hurt you again." Even to himself, his voice sounded rusty and husked .

"I know."

Carmichael fell into step beside him. "Where are you taking her?"

"To my apartment. I can treat her and clean her up. Then we can make further decisions from there."

Much of the stress in Carmichael's face had leached out by the time Renjiro made it to his door. A contingent of the military officers took up position outside the door. He'd only laid her down on the sofa when Carmichael's communicator beeped. "Sir, we have Winstead and Orden in custody."

Carmichael's face settled into a harsh smile. "Excellent. Transfer them to the brig on the ship and await my orders."

"Yes, sir."

Renjiro didn't question the action. He had his own nest to clean out now. He caught Selina with a hard look.

"Carmichael will stay with you. I won't be long."

She opened her mouth to protest, he was sure, before she smiled. "Go. But don't be too long."

She stood in the semi -darkness of the stall, having finally talked Carmichael into letting her rise and shower. Carmichael had filled her in. She knew of the mole in Renjiro's ranks. How they'd found her. None of it settled her anxiety.

Ren would be back soon, she told herself. But during his absence she was tied in knots. "You need to let go of the fear." Saying the words out loud wasn't really enough though.

Instead, she concentrated on the shower. A quick move had the temperature just right and she sighed, letting the aches melt away.

The soothing water sluiced down her sides. She'd fore-gone the offer of a medic, and Carmichael had blustered. Just like he always did. *So predictable.* She snickered quietly as she ducked her head under the liquid.

A sound caught her attention and she peered around the guard , dripping on the tiles. Renjiro was stripping off his uniform. His face set in harsh lines, like his shoulders, and in that instant she realized he'd found his man. Carmichael had indicated it was his second, Jordan. Selina doubted it had been a pleasant or even easy scene.

Perhaps she could raise his spirits a little? A seed of devilry caught her up. He needed something to pick him up. He glanced up and she crooked her finger at him.

His eyes widened then he climbed into the stall, just as she turned around. "Welcome home."

He wrapped his strong arms carefully around her midsection. "I thought you could do with some help soaping your back. If you're up to it."

She laughed. "I could always use help like that. Especially when it comes from a man who looks like you."

He growled in her ear, a playful sound that made her giggle. "You mean only from me."

"Yeah..." Thoughts splintered as his lips found the sensitive spot below her ear, his tongue tickling her slightly. The laughter died away, replaced by a moan as her body warmed. Her breasts tingled and the spot between her legs turned molten. "Oh... Only you, Renjiro."

His hands glided over her wet, hot skin, barely touching. They grazed her breasts and her nipples stood proud, ready for his caress. He tweaked them gently and a bolt of sensation stole her breath. It was pure lightning that streaked through her core. Need pooled within her belly.

"Renjiro, more!" Her quiet demand was met with a deep chuckle .

"For you, my love, I'd do anything. Give you anything." Careful hands now slid down her belly, combing through the thatch of hair to find her vulva, sliding one finger along but not dipping within.

It wasn't enough to fill the void inside. "More!"

He laughed and removed his hands just as she was ready to scream with her frustration.

"Two can tease, my love." Her turn to bedevil him came. She reached back and used her hand, finding his fully erect rod. Before he could stop her, she'd grasped him firmly. The bulbous head was soft and she pressed it with her thumb. He hissed in her ear and she gloried in the knowledge that he wanted her as much as she wanted him. "Now, Renjiro. Don't make me wait."

"Even if I wanted to, I don't think I could." He acted with speed tempered with gentleness. His hands grasped her waist, and he turned her around and lifted her. She gripped his waist with her thighs as he settled her.

Selina felt him at her core, his hardness probed her heat and it was too much. With a squeeze of her thighs she pulled him closer. He plunged deeply. She cried out at the sensation of fullness. Of being one with the man she loved.

His muscles strained and shook as their lips touched. Open -mouthed kisses swallowed their restless cries as the water slid over their naked bodies.

Quickly they moved. He turned, leaning against the cool wall, moving her with fast motions as she arched back, away from him. Needing to feel him within her as much as possible.

Her body coiled tight and the gathering storm within her crashed down quickly. He joined her. Her orgasm spurred his on. Their bodies strained and searched for fulfillment.

For long seconds they hung there, lost in a world of pleasure, before he lowered her back to the stall floor.

"Marry me, Selina. Stay with me forever."

The question surprised her, but she knew there was only one answer. "I will. "

Selina watched as her husband of two hours beamed at the guests. They'd gathered for the celebration on Reunion and she scanned the crowd, wine glass in hand. Their commitment ceremony had been everything she ever dreamed of.

His cousins, Tomi and Kumi, had arrived. Tomi with a gorgeous redhead on his arm. She was a veritable goddess, tall with bright green eyes. And totally dismissive of his much vaunted position.

Kumi, on the other hand, was porcelain perfection with her short, dark bob and chocolaty, almond-shaped eyes. Her looks, like Tomi's, betrayed her Asiatic heritage, as did Renjiro's, but it was clear that Kumi made the most of it.

Carmichael seemed to think she was impressive, if his hot and hungry glances were anything to go by. "You know, I think I should introduce Carmichael to Kumi." She tapped her fingers against her lips.

Renjiro just laughed and shook his head.

Selina turned back to watch the assembled guests once more when a gentle touch caught her attention. "How soon can we leave? We've done all that's been asked—"

She spoke carefully, her stomach churning with knots of concern. How would he react? "After Tomi makes his announcement."

Renjiro frowned."What announcement is that?"

"The one he's just about to make." She indicated with her wine glass as Tomi pushed his way to the front.

"Do you know what this is about?" Ren whispered in her ear as she shivered .

"Why do you think I would know?" The sigh of his breath against her bared skin played havoc with her senses. It was raw need, she acknowledged. Every touch ignited the banked fires that never ceased.

"Whatever it is, I think you already have received the information."

"Hush, my love. Be patient."

He wound his arms around her waist, crumpling the soft white gown she wore. But she didn't care. He was there with her. "I waited five years for you, and that was my limit. I don't do patience very well."

Selina giggled.

Tomi cleared his throat loudly. "Ladies and gentlemen, I'm so pleased you could join us on this happy occasion. Kumi and I welcome our new cousin, Selina, into the Ito Family. As you know, we have a long and proud tradition of serving our people. In the earliest times, our families were warriors and peacemakers. Those who upheld the law. In more recent times, we have made the laws, as members of the senate."

He stopped and Selina waited. She knew exactly what he was about to announce. It was the fulfillment of one of Renjiro's dreams, to join his cousin in the senate.

"Today, I announce that my gift to Renjiro and Selina is a place for my cousin on the Ruling Senate. Renjiro Ito, you have been offered a place among our peers. Say you will join us." Tomi smiled and Selina returned it.

Renjiro stilled behind her, his breath coming faster. "You knew?"

He might have meant his dream or that she knew what Tomi planned. *Have I pushed too far? Too fast?* "I did."

"Thank you." The broken whisper reassured her as did the squeeze. "No other woman would understand."

"No other woman could understand or love you like I do." She turned in his embrace, framed his face, and pulled him close for a kiss that went on forever, to the cheers of the assembled crowd.

PART II

The Assassin

Kumi Ito has her mission, as does Carmichael Snow, but are their objectives compatible?

Kumi Ito is a woman with a problem. Since assuming the role of head of the Commerce Department, she's found discrepancies…the kind that could cause anarchy if the truth got out.

When Carmichael Snow, the commander of the *Emancipation*, comes across intelligence that someone has placed a hit on Kumi, he has to save her. His plan? Hide her and find the assassin.

As they dodge the killer, a passion ignites between them that runs from simmering all the way to steamy. But will the actions of one snatch away their happiness before they can accept what is growing between them?

Chapter 1

Kumi furtively rubbed the aching arches of her feet inside her shoes, wishing the event would come to an end soon. Since she had taken over as the head of the Department of Commerce on Reunion, it felt like she spent more time attending functions than she did in her office. Everyone, it seemed, had to invite her to every damned event. Of course, that was only because the previous head had been socially inclined.

"Now, my dear, you simply must attend the launching of the new flag ship. I'll have my people contact your people." Kumi watched the aging socialite flutter her hands, then took another sip of her wine.

She smiled, more than a little aware of how much her cheeks ached. *That bloody line! It's the bane of my life!*

Back at the office, her tower of files was growing and she was sure her desk was groaning under the piles of data chips waiting. She snuck a discreet look at her timepiece. Three PM. Maybe should could make her goodbyes now? "Hmm." The non- committal groan was enough to allow her to move away.

Kumi headed in the direction of the door, nodding and smiling at the appropriate times. Being an Ito was hard enough, but now that she had the role of head...well, things had become progressively more stifling. The doorway loomed ahead and she surged through it, gulping down the fresh air that whistled through the open window. The Regent, His Highness the Honorable Pasang, was dozing in a chair by the doorway. With great care, Kumi stripped her shoes off and gripped them in one hand. It wouldn't do to wake him. His advanced age was her ally though, and he snored on as she made her escape.

At the front door, the major domo hailed her transport and she shuffled in, pleased to finally take a seat. "To the office, please. Sorry I was gone so long, it can't have been too exciting for you to be waiting around."

"Madam Kumi, after years of this, you learn to find things to do." The driver punched the vehicle into the sky and she relaxed, knowing she'd be at her desk soon enough.

In the distance, she could see the city skyline jutting out above the clouds. Minarets and domes had become the latest architecture craze on Reunion. Many of the larger buildings had refurbished their upper stories to keep up with the style mavens.

The small communicator on her belt gave a cheerful chirp. She was more than happy to answer her personal system. "Kumi Ito."

"Hey, Kumi! Are you busy tonight?"

Kumi rolled her eyes at her brother's teasing tones. "Yes, I am actually. I have reports to read, more than one release to prepare, and—"

"Renjiro and Selina are coming over for dinner. A *family* dinner." She noted the emphasis on 'family' and it caught her interest. Family dinners were usually reserved for announcements. She wondered what that meant, her mind whirring away.

"Hmm. I might be able to make it there for an hour or two, but honestly, there are so many functions..."

Tomi laughed and she frowned.

"Tell me, is it usually like this for you?" Kumi couldn't stop the question from escaping.

"I have excellent executive support. Gillian knows how to get me out of the non-essential functions."

The vehicle was traveling at pace and the building that housed her office was just ahead. "Look, send me details and I'll let you know when I can get there. Oh, and Tomi? Don't ever suggest me for another function like today's. "

"Sure, I'll send you what you need. And on the other? I make no promises." With that the connection faded away.

As the vehicle came to a halt inside the large parking bay, she hustled out and was across the plascrete surface, her mind already delving into the array of problems that needed solving.

At the doorway Dobry, her personal assistant started updating her on various projects. She nodded and smiled, accepting the cup of tea that was handed to her. The rich aroma teased her and she sipped the hot beverage. Once Kumi stepped up to her desk, she slipped the cup onto the tabletop and grabbed the first file.

The report was both comprehensive and disturbing. Selina glanced up and found Dobry waiting, deep frown lines on his face. "So if we don't get the spending on the project perfectly balanced, we run the risk of not being able to finish any of the ships? How could this happen?" Kumi thought it was yet another blow, one that physically stole her ability to think for a moment.

The ships in question were the newest freighters developed to send the foodstuffs Reunion grew in plentiful supply to moon bases scattered throughout the Federation. It was singly the largest source of income for Reunion.

Dobry grimaced. "The previous head... He didn't see that it was a concern. He wasn't very..." The black-haired man stopped and shrugged.

Not for the first time, she felt a burst of pure anger. From everything she'd found in the last few months, her predecessor had been more interested in the social function of his role than the hands-on. Because of his lack of care, Reunion had suffered economically.

At least, very few knew the true state of affairs, she reminded herself. Reunion was teetering on the edge of total financial collapse. Only the senators were aware of how bad the situation really was. If the populace learned... She shuddered. It could result in pure anarchy .

In an effort to repair their shattered economic circumstances, Kumi worked long hours and pared costs to the bone. There was only so much one person could do though. She was grateful that her staff was both efficient and close-lipped. So far, she'd barely scratched the surface of the crisis with their assistance. She had to find a way, needed to formulate a quick but long-lasting plan, to resurrect the economic situation of Reunion.

The information in the cardboard folder before her reinforced her concerns. "Right. Then I suppose we had best get the project managers over here for a meeting. See if we can't find a way to stabilize the credit bleed." With a head shake, she moved the information to the pending pile. It was, by far, the largest mountain on her desk.

Kumi swiped an unsteady hand over her forehead. The constant woes had drained her.

How could the planet's finances have gotten in this kind of mess? She slid into her chair, the padding molding itself to her body.

At times like this, she felt more like a little girl playing grown-up. One who didn't have any answers to the problems. It was overwhelming. Her stomach wobbled precariously then ached. She ignored the discomfort and concentrated on reaching for the next file. *The next disaster.*

"Madam Kumi, it could be worse." Dobry spoke softly and she looked up at him. His face softened as he looked at her . Since she'd assumed her role, she'd become aware of his interest. Kumi hadn't missed his constant cosseting. On one level, she wished she could reciprocate his emotions.

He might be twice her age, but he was steady and very good looking, having dark hair shot with silver and deep blue eyes. He would be, in many ways, the perfect foil for her drive and determination. But she felt no interest in him, except that of a friend. He wasn't the man she yearned for. A quick memory of blond hair and pale, icy blue eyes flashed. She shook herself and thought about his comment.

"I don't see how it could be any worse." She reached for another pile of documents as the communications unit blared. "You set up the appointment and I'll take this comm." She smiled, hoping to soften her dismissal.

With a quick move, she swiveled her chair in the opposite direction. "Kumi Ito speaking."

"Kumi, it's Tomi. We have a problem. I'm en route to your office now."

Her breath caught. What could possibly have happened to make Tomi physically come there? They'd not long spoken.

"Are you all right? Renjiro and Selina?" Her fingers

gripped the communications device, squeezing. Damn it, maybe she was just paranoid, but there'd been things, odd incidents that rattled her. Files disappeared from her system, new budget overruns, strange items turning up in the parking garage. Nothing dangerous, but certainly unsettling. Maybe it was something else. What if people had caught wind of the true financial situation? *Don't go borrowing trouble, Kumi.*

"Yes. Just... Look, Kumi, stay in your office. Don't go anywhere until I get there." Tomi's voice was concerned.

She frowned. "Okay. I'll stay here."

The line disconnected and she stared at the small, silver unit. The call had left her feeling uneasy. It hadn't sounded like her brother at all. Emotions roiled within her. Tomi, the senior senator for Reunion, was usually calm and collected. Nothing ever seemed to shake him. The unusual turn of events did nothing to soothe the burn in the pit of her belly, and unconsciously she rubbed her hand across her stomach.

She opened the line to Dobry's office. "Senator Ito is on his way. When he arrives, we are not to be disturbed." She broke the connection and waited.

Captain Carmichael Snow, commander of the *Emancipation*, watched the man opposite him carefully. Tomi Ito might be one of the most important senators in the Federation, but at this very moment in time, he was also a terrified big brother. His hands were clenched, his knuckles bleached white, and his face was drawn and hard.

The intelligence was explosive. Someone planned to

assassinate Kumi Ito, the head of the Department of Commerce. On a purely visceral level, he felt rage that anyone might attempt to snuff out the life of the wonderfully vibrant woman who'd caught his eye. The fact that he saw it in such a personal light confused him further. Dimly, his psyche demanded that he be more concerned because she was a woman of standing in her community.

He'd kept tabs on Kumi after meeting her at Selina and Renjiro's commitment ceremony last year. She'd... He struggled for the right term. She'd intrigued him.

He turned away, willing himself to focus on the facts as he straightened in his seat. "Until now, she's not said a word about any incidents?" Carmichael's face tightened.

"She's not said a word. I had no idea until one of her staffers apprised me. Then you bring me this." Tomi slumped back in his seat.

"Now that we have this information, we can take steps to protect her, while we hunt for the assassin."

Tomi grunted as he scanned the view. Carmichael couldn't blame him. He considered himself an expert at reading body language. The way Tomi averted his gaze, the stiffness he exhibited... They all spoke of denial and fear. But that wouldn't help Kumi right now. No, at this very point in time, the first thing they needed to do was warn her of the danger, organize a plan for her safety.

"I want you to protect her personally, Carmichael."

The words surprised him. "With all due respect, Senator, my best men will be made available."

"I'm planning to raise this with the regent and the senate leader. I know they would agree that you are the best person to ensure her protection."

Carmichael stared at the man opposite him. *Doesn't Tomi realize? Can't he see? That option wouldn't work, because I want so much more with the woman whose body I would be guarding. She isn't for someone like me.*

Before he could even open his mouth to argue the case, thesenator shook his head. "I don't think I could trust anyone else. I know your background and training. Kumi must be protected. Not just because she's my sister, but because of her role. The work she's doing..." Tomi turned back to glance out the window.

"What do you mean?" The seat squeaked as Carmichael moved, leaning in Tomi's direction.

"There are irregularities within the Commerce Department. She is trying to stabilize the finances of the planet. It's no small feat. We haven't completed our investigations yet, but we are almost..." Tomi shuddered, as if saying the words physically hurt. "We are almost bankrupted. We should have large credit reserves, but they've been frittered away. We're teetering on the edge of disaster."

The back of Carmichael's neck itched. He'd have his men investigate as soon as he had Madam Kumi safely at home. He'd raise his concerns, but first... First, he had to gain her cooperation. She was so bloody independent. He was sure she'd be unwilling to agree without coercion.

The small craft they traveled in approached an imposing tower, slowing and dropping to the plascrete surface with a slight bump, before rolling to a stop in an empty bay. The doors opened and both men climbed out. The glass slider whooshed open and they moved at a pace somewhere between a stride and jog. The silence was welcome. After years onboard the *Emancipation*, he was used to the general hubbub of people. This was still and hushed. The peace before the storm.

A man approached, and he'd guess he was maybe fifty. *He's carefully preserved*, thought Carmichael, noting the impeccable gray suit and discreet adornments. He wasn't tall, but his black hair sprinkled with silver was as immaculate as his clothing. In his uniform, Carmichael felt crumpled before the picture of sartorial elegance. No doubt this was the kind of man Kumi appreciated. He pulled himself up short. He wasn't here to further his relationship prospects. He had a job to do.

"Madam Kumi is expecting you, Senator. Your friend, however..." The man frowned slightly as he indicated with his perfectly manicured hands toward the seating area .

"He is with me."

The man nodded, but his eyes narrowed. "She has requested privacy for your meeting."

Tomi moved through the doorway and Carmichael shadowed him. "Thank you, Dobry."

Carmichael filed the name away. *Never know what will be the piece of information that will solve the puzzle.*

Once inside, the door closed with an audible snick. Behind a large wooden desk overflowing with files was Kumi. As elegant as ever in a silver-gray suit. Kumi wasn't a tall or large woman, but with her golden toned skin and tip-tilted brown eyes she drew attention. Her short, dark hair was worn in a bob that framed her pixie-shaped face.

She looked soft. Womanly. He also knew she had a spine of pure steel. He'd already seen it in action the night he'd squired her at the commitment ceremony.

She smiled as she rose. "Well, Tomi. Whatever this is, it had better be good." Carmichael noted her bare feet with a grin.

Kumi obviously noticed him and his quick glance. She came to a standstill, frowning before stepping in his direction then stopped in front of him. Her gaze dipped to her feet and she blushed the most charming pink tinge along her high cheekbones. "Oh, dear. Do forgive me, Captain." She wiggled the toes which peeked out from under her long, flowing pants.

"There is nothing to forgive, Madam Kumi." He watched her fluid movements and admired her curves. She was sleek and lithe, and his body tightened at the thought of what lay under the light silk jacket.

With a jerky nod, Kumi made for her seat and slowly lowered herself. In a classic move, she folded her hands across the desk, her features now a serene veil of watchfulness. "So then, brother, what's so important that I had to see you immediately and not tonight?"

"It would seem you and your work have been noted by someone with a modicum of power among the Indy rebels. Captain Snow's men intercepted a communication. Kumi, you're making enemies."

She laughed, but it was a mirthless sound. "That's not exactly a surprise, is it? After all, I'm trying to deal with a number of issues." She stopped and looked at him. "Captain Snow, has my brother made you aware of—"

He nodded quickly, cutting off her words. "Yes, he has."

Her smile didn't reach her eyes. "Excellent. Then I had better update you on the status." Tomi scowled at her and Carmichael watched, wondering what she thought she knew.

Tomi exploded. "You knew all along? Then why didn't you…"

Kumi smiled, her eyes lighting up at the obvious outrage on her brother's face and in his mind, the truth dawned. *She thinks we're here because of the financial crisis.*

He sat back to watch the lightning fast discussion

between the siblings. "Tomi, honestly. It's a position I've been training for my whole life."

"You have no idea—"

"Of course I do. The only surprise is that it's taken this long."

"That's not why we are here." Carmichael's voice echoed in the room. Both gazes landed on him.

"What do you mean? That's not why you are here? What other possible reason could there be?" Kumi frowned, the bridge of her nose wrinkling, and her eyes shadowed. He was sure she was reevaluating their exchanges.

"We aren't here to discuss finances or lack thereof."

Kumi sighed and he watched the rise and fall of her breasts beneath the silk. Heavens help him, his groin tightened even more than before at the sight. *Those breasts...* He'd dreamed of her since their first meeting at Renjiro and Selina's union. Since then, he'd seen her several more times. Each encounter reinforced his fascination.

Her face darkened as if her mind was finally whirring into gear. "Captain Snow, that doesn't explain your presence then, does it?" She pierced him with a look.

"No, it doesn't. My men intercepted a communiqué. You are making enemies, as your brother stated. But they don't just want you removed." He sucked in an unsteady breath, pausing as her eyes widened. "They want you dead."

Shock ricocheted through Kumi's body. *Dead?* They wanted to kill her? "But..." Her lips felt stiff as did the rest of her body. Unresponsive. The question hung in the room, like a palpable entity. *How can this be?*

"Kumi, I..." She watched in horror as Tomi rose and Captain Snow—*Carmichael*, her brain interjected—pushed him back into his seat with one hand.

She couldn't understand why he was there. What he was saying couldn't be right, could it? She hadn't heard him rise, hadn't noticed his steps, but now he was there, squatting in front of her. His face was soft and dark. "I won't let them get to you, Kumi. We're going to transfer you to the *Emancipation*." The dark words warmed the cold ache that had taken position somewhere in the pit of her stomach. "They won't get you."

The last words, spoken quietly, snapped her out of the fugue state. "No. I can't run away. That's not the answer."

His blue eyes darkened and his face clenched with a tight, closed hardening of the planes. She blinked away the burning sensation in her eyes. She wasn't some useless piece of fluff, she told herself firmly as she wrestled for control of her emotions.

In the midst of the turmoil, another deep and rich emotion rose. The need to soothe him, to brush away that hard look and the glittering stare, clawed its way to the surface. Confusion fought with concern. She had to stay there and do her job, but a modicum of self-preservation screamed that he'd keep her safe.

"Kumi, you must see sense." His words rasped like sandpaper.

Why? She shook her head. *The why's don't matter. Not now.* The action shattered the crystalline wall of denial that had sprung between them, keeping her separate from him and her brother. *See sense?* A hot rush of frustration and anger coursed through her veins. *He doesn't know what's at stake,* her brain protested. He couldn't possibly know that there was no way she could leave. "I can't. I can't abandon my responsibilities here. The future of so many depends on me being able to do my work. To sort out the issues."

He frowned, and she was sure, he hadn't expected that particular answer from her. "Why?"

Her mouth opened and she shut it with an audible clack. She'd nearly broken her own cardinal rule, the one that said 'keep your own counsel'. It wasn't like her. None of this weakness was. This sense of being disconnected. She wanted to scream and demand he stop whatever magic he was using on her. But it wasn't that. No. The truth was, for the first time ever, she wanted to lean on someone. Let them help her. Not to hide the truth, but to join with her. To fight at her side. To support her.

She shook herself. "I can't explain all the reasons ."

"The planet is financially close to bankruptcy." Tomi's words crashed down on her. They left her cringing over the bald truth.

"Is that right?" Carmichael's words were silky, but held the sting of a knife.

"It's true we are in a bad way..." she hedged. Knowing about the lack of financial stability was one thing, but publicly acknowledging it was entirely different. That could lead to a political uprising. Something no one wanted to even consider.

He stilled, no doubt weighing his words carefully. "Your life is in danger. The best place for you to be is away from here."

She shook her head, denying him an easy out. It wasn't that she wanted to make his job harder, it was just she had the livelihood of everyone on the planet to consider. The truth was, at any time, the people could learn every credit that had been amassed before had been squandered. The far-reaching ramifications froze her belly. Insurrection was days away. Anarchy... *War.*

She turned away from the churning thoughts in her mind. There had to be a better way. "No, Captain. I must stay here. It's my duty."

His lips firmed into hard white lines. For a moment she trembled, wanting to run her fingers along the soft lips she'd remembered in her dreams. She broke away, pulling her gaze from him. *What am I doing?*

She looked sightlessly out the large window. "Find another way. One that doesn't require my absence." In the reflection, she caught sight of her brother's face, screwed up as if he didn't understand what was going on. *Hell, I can barely work it out!* "Tomi, it's fine. I won't do anything dangerous, but you have things to attend to and so, it seems, do I. You head on over to your office. I'll see you tonight."

"Kumi, I shouldn't—"

"Oh, Tomi. What do you think is going to happen? Do you honestly imagine they will get to me while the captain is standing here beside me?"

She knew her voice was waspish, but she needed him to leave. She couldn't cope with him being hurt because he was in the wrong place at the wrong time. Or that she might say the wrong thing and wound him. Sometimes their close bond was as bad as distance.

When she turned back, it was to see him white-faced and worried. "If you go out looking like that, someone will figure it out." She moved quickly, wrapping her arms around him. "You have a job to do just like me. Now put on your senatorial face and go out there. The captain and I... Well, we'll sort this out. I'll be fine with him."

He smiled and one of the millions of tiny little knots inside her snapped away. "If you need me——"

"I'll call." She watched as her brother left the room. Then she was alone with the captain.

———

"**Y**ou can't stay here." Carmichael spoke softly, hoping gentle words would make it easier.

He watched as she turned away, her lips compressed and her arms wound tightly around her body. For an instant, he wondered what it would take to make her lose control. To let her emotions fly. He knew they were there, bubbling away just below the surface. It was one of the things about her that drew him again and again. Her control.

"Nonsense. I have a position here which is integral to my people. I have responsibilities." She'd turned away from him, facing out the window again. He watched the material of her suit float around her body before settling. Since Tomi had left, she'd been quiet, even introspective. He'd waited. She needed time to come to terms with her change in circumstances.

"You also have the right to be safe."

Her shoulders slumped at his words. He didn't want that. What he really wanted was to gather her close, to soothe her fears. *Damn it all!* He wanted that and so much more. He'd never *wanted* with this...this damned ferocity before.

Three quick strides brought him up against her back. He reached out, placing his hands gently on her shoulders.

"I know you want to be here, but right now it's not safe for you. Let me keep you safe."

She laughed, turning her head in his direction. There was no humor in the sound, just anger and frustration. "But it won't be you, will it? It will be some staffer." Her whirling turn sent the soft garment in motion and she gripped the sleeves of his uniform like some damned anchor. He saw the turmoil in her eyes. The fire and anger. "I don't need a bodyguard!"

In that instant, the he knew there could be no other way. "No. It will be me. I will keep you safe."

She tensed below his careful touch. "Why?"

"Because of this." He couldn't have stopped himself even if he'd wanted to. He burned with hunger. It was the starvation of a man for a woman. Of mate for mate. For the one he knew could possibly be the other half of his soul.

Her lips were so close, looked so soft. Where they touched, they yielded beneath his caress. His mind registered them as pillow-like and velvety, succulent and ripe. The thought was ripped away and his arms dropped to her waist, pulling her against him. Her softness strained against the tense muscles of his needy body.

She groaned into his mouth while he devoured and feasted. He felt the convulsive clutch of her hands pulling on his jacket.

His body hardened, going from granite to steel under the onslaught. His senses gloried in her proximity. Then his kiss gentled, and he nipped and tasted while she opened her mouth to him.

When he pulled away, he was as unsteady as she. Her cheeks were rose with a deep blush and her eyes glittered with sexual excitement, while they both breathed heavily. But she remained silent and watchful.

"Well now..." He let his gaze slide away. He cleared his throat, feeling like a teen in the midst of his first encounter, and he cursed himself roundly under his breath.

"So what happens next?"

"What do you mean, what happens next?" He gritted his teeth as he spun on his heel, thanking the plush carpeting for swallowing the sound of his movements. There was a tiny, almost impish smile on her face and he knew right then, he'd seen the first chink in her emotional armor. That woman was both beautiful and exciting.

"I meant, what will you, as my *bodyguard*, do next?" Just as quickly as it bloomed, the smile died away and once more he was faced with the efficient and controlled woman. He wanted another glimpse beneath the facade, but she was locked away again.

"I'd rather you moved away from the window."

"This is my desk, the place where I work. There really isn't anywhere else for me to sit." She gestured to the room and he realized there were piles of files everywhere.

Carmichael growled with frustration, but for now he accepted what she said. *I can open this discussion later.*

He harrumphed, cleared his throat, and indicated Kumi should be seated. "Fine, then let's go through your routine so I know what you usually do."

She took her seat gracefully as if the embrace hadn't happened. His pulse fluttered with disgust at how easily she could throw off the effects while his own body still ached with arousal .

"Okay, let me just bring up my regular timetable." Kumi set to tapping away as he listened to her.

Chapter 2

Kumi and Carmichael entered her tiny apartment through the kitchen. He'd been careful enough to check that no one was waiting inside. It had felt odd and discomforting, the way he'd cautiously pushed the door open, scanned the room, then dragged her inside. He was willing to give his life to save hers. The pressure inside her head built at that knowledge.

The building was fortified and well guarded, he'd informed her, but that didn't mean it couldn't be breached. That information made her shiver, and not in a happy way. The sight of the small laser pistol in his hand, the feral expression on his face... She'd had to turn away, otherwise she wasn't sure she wouldn't tug on him, tell him it wasn't worth it. *She wasn't worth it!*

He'd moved fluidly across the room toward the living area after hissing a "stay here" at her. She'd stayed where he'd instructed, but felt helpless. It was one of those emotions useless feminine creatures gloried in. But that wasn't Kumi. Instead, she reached out, looking for something—anything— that she could use as a weapon. A large, wood-handled spoon hung from a hook by the heater and she gripped it in shaking hands.

"You'd better come back in one piece, Captain Snow!" She couldn't contain her mutter. By the time he returned, she'd been a nervous bundle of energy.

"You're crazy, Snow. I mean who in their right mind—"

"I'm doing my job, princess. In case you forgot, someone wants to waste you faster than a slushy in the heat."

His words made her suck hard on her own pithy comments. After all, there he was risking life and limb to save her. She shouldn't be taking her temper out on him. "I'm sorry. Why don't you sit down and I'll get you a drink. I've got some Venutian Juice or wine. I think I've even got the odd ale in the cooler box."

"No. I need to make contact with my people and set the plans in motion to catch this person." He left the room abruptly while she allowed her gaze to follow him out the door and into the living space beyond.

"Fine then." Gods, how she wanted to brush it off as just a male attribute, but that was lazy and cowardly. Neither a trait she possessed a lot of. She stepped out of her shoes; they'd looked like just the thing to go with her suit, but they'd really been instruments of torture. She lifted them with two crooked fingers and deposited them in the disposal unit with a sigh. "Strike another shoe designer off the list."

As she entered the living area, she noted the way he'd installed himself in one of the overstuffed chairs inherited from her grandparents. She loved those darned seats, the way they made her feel like she was enveloped in their arms. She almost laughed out loud at the flight of fancy, but Captain Snow was hunched in his seat, engaged in a rapid-fire conversation.

"Yes, send me at least a desk unit, some clothing. Yeah, civvies would be best."

His words reinforced her thoughts that he could be there a while. That reminded her to find bedding and set up the spare room for him.

For a second, she allowed herself to dream of coming home to him, his smile, and a loving embrace. She'd had that fantasy before though. She knew it was ridiculous. After all, he was in charge of the *Emancipation*, and she was here, on Reunion. Their work wasn't conducive to any kind of long-term relationship. *Instead of wishing for things that will never come to pass, I'd better tend to his needs.*

She strode into the guest room. It was spartan—little more than a chest of drawers, wardrobe, and bed—but it would at least give him some privacy. She tugged on the bottom drawer, finding sheets and making up the bed. She'd just laid out fresh towels when he entered the room. Now it felt small. Close and intimate.

"Hey. I've got your bed made up, and there are towels right here. Your bathroom is through there." She indicated the small ablution room over her shoulder as she avoided his eyes. His pale, icy orbs seemed to look through to the heart of her. To the emotions she hid. The fantasies she'd entertained about him. Heat pooled in her belly, the same she battled most nights. But here, in a bedroom, it magnified her hunger. The intensity of it nearly blowing her mind.

He didn't say a word, just watched, an inscrutable expression settled on his face.

Her body quaked. She refused to let it show though. Her nipples budded, rubbing against her bra. He kept watching her silently. It felt like the oxygen was being sucked from her lungs and she battled her body's response to his proximity. Her mouth dried.

He took one step. Then another.

"We have... We have to meet with Tomi, Selina, and Renjiro soon. Maybe I should go—uh—change." *Babbling! Gods damn it.* He was reducing her to the mental capacity of a two-year-old. Kumi closed her eyes in self- disgust. She felt a touch, feather light on her cheek.

"Are you okay?"

When she opened her eyes, there he was, staring at her with an intentness that made her want to squirm.

"I know this is difficult, having someone around. Believe me, I understand. But..." He spoke quietly while her brain spun its own web of questions.

Maybe if she just took the initiative? Showed him what she wanted. If he brushed it off...well, then she knew exactly where she stood, didn't she? If he responded, then she could work him out of her system.

He was still talking, and she watched, fascinated at the way he used his hands to make a point. Heat crept along her cheeks.

I can do this. After all, it's just sex, right? Sexual hunger that I can work off then forget. It doesn't mean anything. She ignored the part of her brain that told her it was so much more. That she was an idiot. That if he pushed her away, he'd leave and send another to do the job.

She closed her eyes, gathering her confidence around her, and sucked in an unsteady breath. With a groan she threw herself at him, wrapping her arms around his shoulders. "It's not having just someone. It's you."

She fixed her lips on his, felt the stillness of his form before it melted away and his arms encircled her. He pulled her closer and she felt the heat emanating from him.

Their lips clung to each other's. Her hands roamed over his chest, learning the dips and hollows, tracing the hard pectoral muscles and continuing their mad foray. Fingertips played with the clips of his uniform jacket and, without thought, she plucked at them, hearing the pop of buttons as they hit the carpeted floor.

His mouth moved, skating along her jawline, and nibbled its way to her ear. Her chest moved rapidly, sucking in any oxygen she could get, while he worked the most amazing magic on her system.

Carmichael's hands found the loose jacketed top and slid underneath, burrowing to slide over the skin of her belly. It quivered in reaction and she arched back, needing more of his touch. "Oh. Please. Carmichael." Her broken words filled the air. She hunted blindly and tugged on the buttons of her jacket before she thrust it from her shoulders, knowing she'd die if he didn't fill her soon.

Her bra was removed with an efficient move from the sexy captain.

"I've dreamed of you." His rough words hit her hard in the solar plexus just as his fingers closed over her breasts, tugging the material until it tore. "The nights I've dreamed of filling you. Of drinking you and sucking your breasts like this." He bowed his head and took the small bud into his mouth. Sensations of lightning streaked through her and she cried out. Her fingers settled in his hair, pulling his head closer so he'd take more.

Carmichael's fingers found the waistband of her pants and his fingers dove deep, just finding the damp hairs at her center when the jangle of a communications device split the air.

She stiffened, aware that at any second, with a small move he'd have them within her aching empty core. But they remained still, listening as the answering service kicked in.

"Hey, Kumi. Are you still coming around? Ren and Selina have just arrived. If you can't, let me know, otherwise I'll worry."

Tomi! She closed her eyes, willing her heart rate to settle and her body to stop throbbing with the hunger.

Finally, Carmichael raised his head. "This can't... This won't happen again." He'd pulled away from her emotionally as well as physically, stripping out of his jacket and holding it out to her, while he averted his gaze.

She could see the fine tremors in his hand. Tears welled in her eyes, but she blinked them away. "No. No, it won't."

Kumi accepted his jacket and pulled it around her. "I'm going to shower and dress. Ring Tomi. Tell him we'll be there soon." Then, with the remains of her shredded dignity wrapped around her, she left him.

The stilted atmosphere in the room was pure torture. Kumi avoided Carmichael's eyes and kept as much physical distance between them as possible. Selina kept watching him as if expecting a second head to grow, Tomi was frowning, and only Renjiro was smiling.

The food probably tasted delicious, but to be honest, he couldn't even recall what he ate. How could he? She was sitting beside him, but might as well have been a million miles away.

"So you have news?" Kumi placed her fork down on the plate .

"We do. In fact, it's news for all of us. Tomi, would you like to go first though? You are, after all, the head of our family." Her cousin, Renjiro, had lately been made a senator for their planet, but while his designation might have changed, his attitude toward life hadn't. Right at this second, Renjiro looked proud and Carmichael noted the faint smile on Kumi's face as well as the broad grin on Selina's.

Renjiro as a senator and Selina as a senator's wife seemed incongruous. In Carmichael's formative years, the only contact he'd had with senators was when they came to bestow their presence on those from his village or to lecture on the importance of the Federation, something which happened with surprising regularity at his small country school. What he hadn't learned about the history of the Federation and Reunion in school he had learned during his years in the Federation Navy.

The federation of planets had been formed three centuries before, in order to give the human colonists a protective power base. They'd believed in the adage of power in numbers. Those that didn't join became the Independent Planets. But their independence had come at a high cost as hostile aliens encroached. Unable to protect themselves and their people, they had entered negotiations with the Federation. There had been resistance though. Pockets of resistance mobilized to destroy what had been achieved.

Reunion had been one of the first planets to join the Federation, and there were families with long and glorious traditions of serving in the Senate. The Ito family was foremost. Even he, a farmer's son and now naval captain, understood their importance.

When Tomi Ito cleared his throat, Carmichael tugged

himself back from his thoughts. "Captain, as you are aware, the relationship between planets and the Naval Command is very close. I have been duly deputized by the Naval Commission to inform you that the *Emancipation*, with you as captain, is to be permanently reassigned and stationed on Reunion, effective immediately."

His chest tightened at Tomi's words. "Here?"

He'd never considered that they'd place the *Emancipation* here. On Reunion. Until now, the naval ship hadn't been associated with any home-world. His beleaguered mind whirred slowly back to life. He had more than his fair share of officers and enlisted men from the planet. Maybe he should have guessed it was coming. But the truth was he hadn't.

Reunion. He didn't know if he should view it as a promotion or demerit.

The congratulations flowed around him and he snuck a quick glance at Kumi. She kept her face composed. Her eyes, though, were shadowed, as if she was trying to find a way to forget the announcement. That cut him all the way to the core. The ache radiated and it took several minutes of careful breathing to bring it under control.

"You said there was other news?" Kumi cocked her head to one side and he watched, fascinated, knowing the whole time she was attempting to ignore him and his study of her.

Selina and Renjiro grinned broadly. "Well, since our favorite people are here..." Selina giggled, and he watched in amazement as the hard-nosed, ex-freighter captain smiled and her face transformed with a radiant glow.

"What my wife is trying to say is, we're going to be parents."

The chorus of congratulations rose several decibels and Kumi stretched forward to hug Selina.

"Carmichael and Kumi, we want you to be the child's Cultural Guardians. We know you will do the right thing, take care of him or her should anything happen to us." Selina's eyes were watery. "Please say you will, Carmichael and Kumi."

A lump formed in his chest. *CG? It is the ultimate in trust. That any parent... That Selina and Renjiro, with his whole extended family...* His mind boggled at the honor. Then it occurred to him that it would tie he and Kumi together. Forever.

The news wasn't exactly unexpected, Kumi reflected on the way home in the vehicle with Carmichael. *Captain Snow*, she corrected herself. Selina and Renjiro had been officially paired for over a year. As to the other ...well, she could ignore that. Maybe. So long as she didn't have to see him too often. She glanced out the window, the fiery glow of day muted to the deep shadows of night.

They were just coming in to land on the pad when a ping and a clunk were followed by a loud bang. The air-car wobbled a little and she reached out, gripping the secura-straps. Her horrified gaze settled on Carmichael's face. She expected him to grin in the superior fashion and tell her there was nothing to worry about. Instead of that, his face looked taut in the glow of the instrument panel. Anger, shock, and concern washed over her.

The vehicle shuddered. "Something's hit us, hasn't it?"

"Yesss," he hissed, jerking on the controls as their transport nosed down. "Brace yourself, I'm not sure I can hold this."

A whine started, it split the air while the rapid beeping of instruments reinforced just how precarious their situation was. Her heart lodged in her throat, and though she wanted to scream, she bit her lip, trying to hold it in.

It felt like forever, but it couldn't have been more than seconds as he cursed and swore, pulled and fought. The craft bucked and rolled wildly. Kumi was sure she'd be sick, but she held on tight as the asphalt rose to meet them.

The landing was rough, jarring them both hard. Afterward, she sat there blinking. "Carmichael? Are you okay?" She reached for the snaps of her belt, her chest and shoulder aching where the webbing had pulled tight . He didn't answer.

Finally free, she turned back in the seat, her eyes wide open. "Carmichael? Please, you're scaring me."

"We have to get out of here." He wrenched on his belts, tearing them from his body, his voice hoarse and low. "You're okay, aren't you?"

"Yes."

"Good, then we have to move. At least we're near your building." He shoved against the door, and it squeaked, but refused to move.

The tiny car shook. An acrid tang rose. She knew that smell.

"Smoke." A bubble of panic clogged her lungs and hysteria almost overwhelmed her. She pushed the emotions away and reached for her door. It didn't budge. "Carmichael, how do we..."

In the short period of time she'd been working on her door, he'd freed himself from his seat and levered his legs up. "Cover your face."

"What?" She complied, tugging the light jacket over her head.

Bang!

His hands pulled at the garment. "We need to hurry."

The licking tongues of fire crept along the length of the vehicle, but she watched as he turned and scrambled out the windscreen before reaching for her. "Come on."

She reached for her bag. "I just need—"

"We don't have time." He gripped her hand tightly and tugged.

She fell among the glass strewn metal of the front of the vehicle. The scrapes and cuts hurt a little, but she ignored them as they tumbled to the asphalt.

Winded, she looked back, noting that the back of the air -car now glowed. "Oh my gods!" Moving was instinctual. They rose, pushed away from the radiant heat, and then scrabbled to their knees and up. The door looked so far away, but they pumped their legs, hoping to gain safety while her lungs ached.

She didn't have time to question anything as the sound and shockwave tore through her clothing, lifting both herself and Carmichael like kites on the wind. The shock thrust them against a wall and held them there for an instant before letting them drop with sickening thuds. Heat and pain clawed at her, but she refused, absolutely refused, to give in to the gray-black which filled her sight.

"Car... Carmichael?" She realized he was on the ground, slumped beside her.

She willed her body to move, an inch. Her fingers flexed. She reached, touching the bleeding skin of his hand. "Don't be dead."

He groaned and never before had she felt so drunk or giddy at a sound.

Noises filled her consciousness. The sound of thudding footsteps, the crackle of flames. Screeching, groaning metal. She focused on the people who crowded around.

"Are you okay?"

"Call a medic."

Hands touched her. "I'm okay. Him. He needs treating."

Kumi made to stand, but gentle hands kept her still. "Wait until the medic has checked you. He's awake too, so no doubt they'll check both of you out."

Groping in her pockets, she found her communicator, depressing the button. "Tomi? It's Kumi. I need you."

<hr>

Carmichael's body ached. In fact, it was safe to say he was one big ache. The bed in Kumi's spare room might be comfortable enough, but right now, he couldn't tell. The medic from the *Emancipation* ran the wand over his nude body. The clothing he'd been wearing was little more than rags. It'd been torn, scorched, and bloodied.

"Captain, I don't have to tell you how lucky you are." The loud words left him wincing.

"I'm glad to be lucky, rather than slightly unlucky."

The medic opened his small cache of medications with a long-suffering sigh.

"What are you giving me?" He frowned and groaned as even that taxed his bruised body.

"A light analgesic is about all you need. I'm also going to prescribe a sonic bath and some skin spray. We need to be sure you have no foreign particles and that will seal your abrasions."

"Good. Once that is attended to I can—" He started to

rise up on his elbows, but the firm hands of the doctor pushed him back against the pillows. He sucked in an unsteady breath as more than a twinge assailed him. His stomach roiled, and he fought the nausea as he accepted the welcoming embrace of the bed.

"Not so fast, Captain." The too loud voice made his head ache, or it could have been the result of his movements. He didn't plan on investigating that too closely right now.

"Madam Kumi..." He closed his eyes, knowing that right now he wasn't much use to anyone.

"Is fine by the looks of it. I'll see once I'm finished here. She looks a darned sight better than you. To be honest, you're incredibly lucky to have got ten off as lightly as you did."

Intellectually, he was aware of that. They'd been lucky to survive the attack. He'd bet his money on a light range missile being the cause of the damage to the vehicle. That meant the assassin had started his or her job and was close by.

Tomi and Kumi had somehow managed to hustle him inside, and the major domo had overridden the lifts to get them to her apartment with speed. The knowledge didn't soothe him. Tomi had contacted his ship. His second arranged to have men shuttled down to ensure that Kumi was protected at all times, but it made him feel damned useless.

Frustration filled him. It was his *job* to protect her. He didn't accept failure well, and right now it rode him hard. If he were honest with himself, this mission was more than just a job. This was *Kumi* he was protecting. He uttered a harsh swear word.

"You know, it's not so bad. By tomorrow you should be up and around, Captain."

"That's not enough. I need to be out of here tonight. Back—"

"Captain, you are many things—brave, loyal, honorable. Remember, I've seen you in battle. But if you get out of that bed, then I will have to add one more adjective to my list."

He grunted, attempting to ignore what he was sure would be said next.

"I'd have to add hard headed. You aren't in any condition right now to protect anyone. Give it two or even three days and you'll be sufficiently recovered, with the help of these sprays. But if you ignore my advice..."

Carmichael knew what the man was saying was correct, but it still chapped his rump. He tugged the coverings up over his waist with an absent flick.

"Right, almost done here."

He felt the tingle of the application against his skin just as a knock came at the door. "Enter." Carmichael made to brush the irritation of the hypo-syringe away, much to the grunted dismay of the medic.

The door swung wide and Kumi stood there. Even at this distance, he could tell she'd been crying. Her eyes were red-rimmed. The bubble of fear that had lodged in his heart shifted.

"I came to see how you were getting on." Her chin wobbled a little, as if she were barely holding it together.

"Madam Kumi, I was just coming to—" The medic frowned, and Carmichael wished he could throw him out on his ear while he checked to see how bad her injuries were.

"I'm fine." She stepped inside and closed the door.

Doesn't the damned woman realize I'm naked?

The part of him that seemed to always react when she was near, stood to attention. He nearly blushed, but instead he concentrated on reciting the articles of the Treaty of Destutin in his head.

"No, you're not fine. You've got some nasty cuts and abrasions with a fair bit of dirt in them and a whopping bruise on your arm."

The look she threw at the medic could have frozen icebergs. He saw the way Kumi's eyebrows drew together and her lush lips flattened as she swung in his direction.

"I just... I just wanted to thank you. For saving me, I guess." She turned away and he noted the charred edges of her perfect bob. "I didn't really think it was serious before. I'm sorry. I should have listened."

He raised a hand and she took it. A bolt of pure erotic electricity shot through him from the top of his head to the ends of his toes.

In that moment, he understood the truth. He'd die for this woman. She was the only one he loved.

Kumi grimaced as she dressed. In the days since the air-car had been shot down, she'd agreed to every restriction Carmichael placed on her. She hadn't left the apartment without adequate protection—that is what *he* deemed appropriate—but three burly security officers had felt like overkill, not that she'd complained about it. Never again would she argue with him. The fright of the attack on the air-car had stilled her heart. Both fear and panic had assailed her in that instant. Yes, that and one other emotion—loss.

He'd been prepared to die for me. Her stomach cramped, just as it did each time that thought rose. She'd restricted her interaction with others to the bare minimum, her work being delivered to her door by courier. It wasn't the way she liked to conduct her business, but she'd tolerate the need to stay out of sight.

She tapped away on her screen, scrolling through the information, requesting clarifications from Dobry. But tension crackled in the small apartment. It had been the same for days.

"Dobry, when will I receive the updated costings on the freighters?"

In the viewing screen, he grimaced. "Not until later, Madam. But... If you came in, you could access all the information I have on hand."

"I can't. Not yet. I have some personal issues , as I've explained." She gritted her teeth. Dobry had become more insistent, but so far she'd been able to give him the carefully prepared excuses. It wouldn't last too much longer. He or someone else would begin to question why she hadn't been anywhere near her office. "Just send me what you have." She clicked off the viewing screen and sat back, her hands steepled on the heavy wood desktop.

"I'm not sure this plan is going to work." Carmichael's voice filtered down the hall from his bedroom. She'd barely even entered there since the medic had left. They'd nearly... She cut off the thought as she concentrated on the sounds.

"There has to be a link somewhere." The voice of his officer was angry and tired. She knew many of them were working around the clock to find out who and why the attack had taken place.

Kumi strained to hear the conversation. His people had

been coming and going with increased monotony and the greater his mobility the more had arrived at her door.

"Well, there are problems from what I understand, vast economic issues relating to Reunion. I need you to follow those through. Investigate whether they might have some bearing on the hit that has been ordered against Madam Kumi."

Her breath fled. Could that be it? Could it really be that simple? She waited as she slipped her hands under her legs. She tossed the ideas over in her head. *It's like a puzzle, a pastime I've always been found intriguing. Dealing with the economy is like completing a puzzle. Can this be the same?*

She rose from her seat, hating the squeak that gave her away. For the first time, she cursed the ancient furniture she'd received from her family, but the conversation didn't slow or halt. Her stealthy footsteps took her closer to the wall and doorway.

"I need this cleared up quickly, Major." His words reminded her that he was there for a short while, only to capture the person or persons who wished her dead. "I will not waste my life hunting down some petty criminal while Reunion rots away beneath my feet."

Her guts clenched. Hard. *He doesn't want to be here? On Reunion? Why not?* Her brain whirled madly. It wasn't as if this planet was some dark end of the universe. He could still run his ship and...

She forced her mind to consider, objectively, the situation. *He never promised anything, and dear gods, the one time I nearly got him where I wanted him, he backed off at a million miles an hour!*

Kumi stepped back away from the wall. She didn't want or need to hear anymore. There was a sensation in her chest that she'd never felt before. Cold and heavy with jagged edges, or maybe it was her heart, splintering. Either way, it stole her breath. Ungainly footsteps took her to the desk and she gripped it hard, glad for the stable surface as her knees wobbled. Her glance out the window took in nothing of the shining , sunny day. Instead, she fought to control the pain.

He doesn't love you. He never will. The truths battered her while she gasped into the silent room. She raised a hand to her mouth, hoping to muffle the sounds she made. *After all, it's not like I...* In that instant, knowledge of her own feelings flared. *I love him.* Kumi bowed her head under the onslaught of the intense emotions. *I love him. He doesn't love me.*

"Then I guess I will just be wedded to Reunion." She pulled her hand away, gulping heavily before muttering the words, trying them out for size.

It wasn't enough. It would probably never be enough. She would prepare herself for a long, lonely life, fussing over Renjiro and Selina's children. And any Tomi had too. She could be the fabulous spinster aunt instead, who entertained the children and then gave them back. It was an empty future which stretched out before her.

One breath. Another. She had to rein herself and her emotions in before he came out and found her. It wouldn't be long. She needed control.

The burn on her cheeks had settled to a deathly cool, but she accepted it. "I won't embarrass myself." Then she made her way to her seat, reengaging her computer. No, she'd work her way through the pain.

Chapter 3

Carmichael glanced in Kumi's direction. She'd been silent and almost withdrawn since he'd seen his tactical officer out of the apartment. It wasn't any one thing he could put his finger on. She answered him when he questioned her, but the answers came in short bursts. Instead of her intense glances, she barely even turned in his direction and focused almost entirely on the screen in front of her.

He stalked the length of the room. Stopped. Ran his fingers through his short hair then turned. Paced back to the other end of the room. "Tell me about the financial crisis."

He watched the way she stilled. "What particularly do you wish to know?"

Her gaze slid over his shoulder and he controlled the urge to turn and see the report she'd been reading. "How did this occur?"

Her head tilted, and for an instant he was reminded of a bird he'd once seen—the way it had watched him, as if weighing what his action would be. "Do you think this has bearing on the rest of your mission?"

"I don't know. But what I do know is we need to catch whoever is behind the hit. And soon." He turned and strode to the end of the room, dropping down into a chair with a sigh. His body was healing, but slower than in the past. The medic had explained his age was a factor. Getting older was a bitch.

"I honestly don't know where to start." She lounged back into her chair. "When my predecessor finally left, we started to discover that everything was really a house of cards. With one puff, everything will fall down."

"So, how does that affect the Federation?" He closed his eyes, ready to let her soothing , melodic voice wash over him while he continued sorting through the facts in his head.

"Reunion is the jewel in the Federation crown. It was one of the first signatories, but you already know that. Each of the first planets had a role, and ours was to be the food bowl for the Federation. Being a mainly agrarian planet, our people knew how to work with the land and had the oceans to harvest the best yields. Other planets were mining or centers of learning."

"So, when you discovered the truth about the financial situation? What about how the people would react?" He watched as she shivered a little at his words.

"It would be a serious blow to the Federation. We have so little credit left. I'm trying to find a way to replace our aging fleet of freighters. We really can't afford it, but we need the income. If it were common knowledge..." She broke off, swiping an unsteady hand over her forehead.

Financial terrorism. It wasn't anything new. In fact, it reminded him of the plot that had nearly seen Selina die the previous year. The Indies had plotted to blow up the Moon Base. What if it was tied to that? His mind began examining the information for linkages.

"Do you have any Indies on your payroll? Anyone with connections?"

The high whine of a laser split the air, the sound shrill, and his instincts took over. He rolled to the floor with an *oomph.*

"Get down!" He started crawling along the floor in her direction. Shards of high performance glass littered the floor, making his movements slow as he avoided further injury.

He reached the chair, his hands latching around her ankles. "Kumi? Gods damn it, Kumi, answer me." There was no answer, and for a moment his mind splintered. *What if she was...*

Anger and fear threatened to steal his thoughts. He tugged her chair and pulled her supine form down to him. She was still, yet breathing, he noted as she lay in his arms, her eyes closed. He couldn't see any blood and gave thanks for the small mercy .

Carmichael ran his unsteady hands over her body, checking for an injury. It was only when he ran his fingers through her silky, soft hair that he found the knot and the oozing blood. He needed to get her out of there. *Watch for concussion.* The sound of his blood coursing in his veins flooded his senses while in his chest, his heart beat rapidly.

He reached for his communicator as the door burst open. Three of his security team, wearing their black tactical uniforms and clutching their P-37 laser rifles, hurried in his direction. It was like slow motion. Each step brought them nearer to where he was huddled on the floor with Kumi.

"You're fine, sir?"

"Yeah. But Madam Kumi is hurt. Get me a gods damned shuttle. I want her out of here right now." His rough words set one of the men moving into action while the other two conferred.

"They're gone. The men on the roof have advised they pursued, but the assailant eluded them. They did, however, find something. They are retrieving and heading in our direction."

He nodded, feeling helpless. He'd failed again. And Kumi was injured.

She moved and groaned in his embrace. "What... What happened?" Her eyes opened , and for the moment he lost the ability to speak. She was the most glorious creature he'd ever seen. Her soft weight and glowing eyes reaffirming his reason for living.

"You got hurt. There was an attack. Kumi, we have to get out of here."

She raised a hand to her head, but he intercepted it, held it gently. "My head aches. How did I get hurt?"

He shook his head. "Not now. Once we're out of here and you've been checked by a medic then we'll discuss what happened."

She opened her mouth and he knew she was about to refuse. Unable to help himself, he laid his finger against her mouth. The explosion of nerves stealing what was left of his common sense. He needed to kiss her. So he did, leaning in and laying his lips against hers. It wasn't explosive or wild. It was more like a promise and a vow. It was more powerful than any other caress he'd ever shared.

When he pulled back, he studied her face. She was shocked. Her face white and pinched. Kumi closed her eyes and he felt the distance between them. "No. Not ever again." She pushed against his chest. "I won't do this again. I won't fall for you so you can break my heart."

He wasn't sure if he should be elated or alarmed. Instead, he focused on getting her out of danger.

"I'm such a fool." Now that the medic had left, Kumi could lever herself up. Her head spun, but she needed a shower to wash away the grime and fear that coated her skin.

Slow and unsure, she worked at the buttons on her tunic top. It was a pity really, she liked this top, but it was shredded and stained. She wadded up the material and thrust it into the waste receptacle, pleased that the young ensign had already delivered a uniform for her to wear. It wasn't perfect and it wasn't hers, but it was clean, and that was good enough.

She tugged at her bra, thankful she was small enough for a front closing garment. It fell to the floor and she sighed as the cool air swept over her newly naked skin. Dipping her fingers down the waistband of her pants, she pushed, catching her panties as they moved over her hips with a shimmy.

The walk to the ablution room was only a matter of steps and she slid the door open before she closed it after herself.

"Water. Warm. Full spray." Stepping into the shower stall left her moaning as the beat of water hit her head and shoulders. There was pain, but her muscles relaxed. Kumi pushed her hands against the wall and dropped her head, welcoming the sensations. How long she stood there she wasn't sure, but when she finally gave the instructions for the water to cease, the throb in her head had subsided slightly.

The towel she'd spied on the hanging rail was within reach and she extended her arm, closing her hand around the thick material. It was a luxury in space to bathe with water, so she must be in one of the VIP units. She snorted. It didn't really matter if it was. She was there to be kept safe. Not because Carmichael wanted her close by. That much had been made brutally clear as he'd disappeared within minutes of depositing her on the bed.

The medic had come by, done his thing, and applied a healing spray to her head, telling her to rest.

Carmichael hadn't returned. She hoped he hadn't heard her words back on Reunion though. The ones where she all but told him she loved him. That would have been the ultimate in embarrassing gaffes.

"It isn't like you aren't already good enough at embarrassing yourself and everyone else. First you nearly strip him naked and jump on him in the bedroom, and then you eavesdrop and realize he doesn't want you. And just in case you missed it, he doesn't want any association with Reunion."

Kumi stopped toweling herself dry to look in the mirror. Staring back was a woman in her late twenties. Her short hair hung in wet strings that plastered to her face like thick, dark, wet noodles. Her skin was bronzed and she checked her lean features. Her eyes were almond-shaped and dark, shadowed. The beginning of lines had taken up residence on her face. *They're new.* She raised a shaking hand to push against them. "Welcome to the world of growing older, Kumi."

With a heavy sigh, she turned back to the door and

pushed it open, only to stop short at the sight that met her eyes.

There was Carmichael, waiting for her. He'd collected up the pile of clothing she'd carelessly left on the floor. Her mouth dried as his eyes ran up and down her almost nude body. Things down below tingled and she clamped her legs together firmly. It didn't do her any good though, a spike of desire wound through her veins.

His face was turning ruddy as if him being caught there was somehow her fault. Bravado was the only way out of this, she told her sluggish mind. "What are you... What do you want, Captain?" She tugged the towel closer as her nipples budded ; sensations pulsed deep within her body.

"What do I want?" He parroted the words back to her, and a lump took up residence in her throat.

"Yes. Why are you here in this cabin?" She would swear her voice sounded breathless, but he didn't seem to notice. She licked her lips.

"Damn it, Kumi. I'm here because..." His voice died away and he held out a hand. Heaven only knew, she wanted him to touch her, but if he did, surely she would go up in flames. The heat and longing rose, just like it always did whenever he was around. Only this time she didn't have her armor in place. The only thing she wore was the damned towel.

"Kumi, I... I came to see if you were okay." His voice was strangled, and for a moment she was sure there was a glimpse of something more in his eyes.

"I'm fine, as you can see." She stood still while her body cried out for him. Each passing second eroded another small bit of the barrier she'd reinforced around her heart.

"I'm glad." He took a step forward.

Her stomach wobbled and she nearly stepped back, away. His gaze ran over her naked shoulders, stopped for an instant at the swell of her breasts then flicked away to the wall. Her body flamed hotter.

"I'm so damned glad." He stepped again, until he was against her. Tall and muscular , this blond-haired, blue-eyed man. "You have no idea just how glad." Then he kissed her.

"What have you learned?" The major stood at the tactical desk while Carmichael took a seat.

"Sir, we have retrieved the item. It looks like an electronic address book. There is no identifying information though. I have the boys going through the encryption now. The only other thing is that we think one of our guys winged the assassin. We found blood on the ground under the point where we believe the air bike was stationed. The men have taken scrapings. The downside is that it's a public access -way. So we'll have to decontaminate the DNA before we can begin to match the genetic sequence. Senator Ito has cleared access to the global DNA banks so we can type and match as quickly as possible."

Carmichael listened in silence, knowing that the whole time he was talking to Major Bortheays the medic was closeted with Kumi. She was in the best possible hands, but it didn't make him feel any better. He wanted to be with her, but he'd drawn the line in the sand. *He'd said ever again.* He'd never before regretted an outburst like that one. It felt like his chest had been cleaved into two pieces. He was sure he'd left part of himself with Kumi.

"What about the other line of inquiry we discussed earlier?" Carmichael stood and turned to face the wall, stopping himself from checking his wrist unit. It had to have been fifteen, maybe twenty minutes since the medic had arrived.

"Sir, I've got men looking into the department itself, the leaks and even checking through the communications system. I'm about to send some more out to work on gathering the communications records of everyone in the building."

When he turned back to the major, he frowned at the concern on the man's face. "What?"

"We'll find them, sir. They will regret harming her. You have our word."

They knew. They all knew. How could they? "What do you mean?"

"Sir, we know you. We've served together for many years. You don't react like this unless it's important to you. Unless this person, Madam Kumi, is important to you. It won't go past my teams. But we wanted you to know. We'll get them."

His fingers clenched and his leather gloves squeaked. He gave a jerky nod. "Fine. Thank you, Major."

He turned on his heel and made to the door. He stopped, nearly turned , and told him they were wrong. That he didn't love Kumi. But he couldn't. He couldn't deny the emotions that battled so deep within. So he left the office without another word.

What to do? He could go to his office —there were always plenty of reports to finalize—but he was walking back to her cabin. In the hallway, he caught up with the medic.

"How is she?"

"Captain. I'm so glad to catch you. She'll be fine. I've treated her and she has received the anti-concussive hyperspray. She'll be sore for several days and probably have a headache for a day or two, but will make a full recovery. You should let me check you over."

"No. I'm fine." He verbally flicked away the medic's concern.

"Captain..."

"I'm fine. Is she up for visitors?"

The medic nodded.

Carmichael smiled. "I'll check in on her then. Thank you."

The stiff inclination of the medic's head told him he wasn't happy with Carmichael's decision. Carmichael waited until the medic was out of sight.

The door opened on Carmichael's command. The room was empty, but his eyes landed on the pile of clothing littering the floor. As the door closed behind him, he bent over, scooping the discarded garments up. They were still warm from lying against her skin and carried her scent. He inhaled deeply, letting her essence fill his senses. A sense of deja vu filled him.

As he exhaled, he noted the door opening to the ablution room. Then she was there, her damp hair framing her fine features. Her almond-shaped eyes were dark, and his stomach cramped. He'd come so close to losing her. His face flame d as he realized all she wore was the towel. It was the only thing hiding her beautiful body from his hungry gaze .

"What are you... Again? What do you want, Captain?" She stumbled over the words, obviously as surprised as he was. He watched as she tugged on the towel, but it highlighted the curves of her body, and his own heated with desire.

"What do I want?" He wanted to scream at the inanity of his own comments, but held onto the tiny shred of control that hadn't yet fled.

"Yes. Why are you here in this cabin?" He watched as she licked her lips. A groan rose in his throat.

"Damn it, Kumi. I'm here because..." Was there any way he could swallow the words he'd said to her in that bloody bedroom? Any way he could tell her just how much he regretted his outburst?

"Kumi, I... I came to see if you were okay." His voice was strangled with the mass of emotions that grew in his chest. He needed to save her. To love her. To hold her. To make whoever would hurt her pay.

"I am, as you can see." She blinked, and he knew then she wasn't as unaffected as she made out.

Time to take a chance. "I'm glad." He took a step forward. His gaze ran over her naked shoulders, noting dimly that heaven was only as far away as she was. "I'm so glad."

He raised his gaze to her eyes. "You have no idea just how glad." Then he kissed her.

<hr>

The feel of his lips on hers was electrifying. It made her yearn for things she'd pushed away. The emptiness she felt, the need to feel the pleasure of a man's touch. This man's touch specifically. That wasn't all, but the rational part of her brain scolded her. *He doesn't want me. He told me that.* Her heart hungered for his touch.

She gave in, melted into the warmth of his embrace

when his arms rose to circle her waist. Her nerveless fingers lost their grip on the towel, but she didn't even realize, lost in the wonder of rising sensations. Their lips sipped and mated. Her hands rose, fingers buried in his golden hair.

The ache in the pit of her belly reminded her of the emptiness. That only he could satisfy her needs. She shivered and his hands moved, warming her at each pass.

"Carmichael, I want you."

He groaned into her mouth, his touch firmer and surer. His fingers burrowed beneath the gaping towel, finding her curves hidden from view.

When his hands rose into the short hair to tug her head back, she yelped with pain and sprang away.

"Oh gods! What am I thinking?" He stepped back, leaving her nude body icy cold. He scrubbed unsteady hands over his face and inside her the tiny light that had started to glow guttered out.

"Get out!" Tears stung her hands and she groped for the towel, pulling it up to cover her form.

"What? No! I thought I'd hurt you." He stalked forward, but she tried to turn away, covering herself with scrabbling hands on the towel.

She didn't want to see the disgust on his face. Better she not look, she told herself. "Please, just go. I can accept that you don't want me, but don't make this harder."

She couldn't look him in the face. Twice she'd tried and twice she'd failed. Surely now she knew and could leave him alone. Her skin burned with shame. Tears dribbled down her face, scorching her cold skin.

His hands touched her shoulders, turning her. "I want you. I always have." But she heard a hesitance in his voice.

"You're just trying to save me from humiliating myself. That's terribly noble, but I'd rather get dressed and—"

"You're not going anywhere. I'm not planning on letting go of you now." He pulled her close, but she remained stiff in his embrace. "Kumi, I thought it was best to let you go. Until the attack. Then I realized I can't. There's..."

She waited. "*What?* Carmichael, tell me the truth. Nothing more and nothing less."

"I can't ever let you go. Couldn't even if I tried. When I saw you there, in the chair, my heart stopped, Kumi. It made me face the truth, that I can't ignore my feelings. Whether you feel the same or not. I love you, Kumi."

Her gaze flicked up and met his. *He's serious.* There wasn't a scrap of laughter or concealment. No, his emotions were all over his face for her to read.

"But you said..." Could she trust him? Her heart said yes, but her brain urged caution.

"I did. I said that. Never have I hated myself more. If I could take the words back I would. I'd swallow them. It was never my intention to hurt you, but I did."

She raised a shaking hand, laid her palm against his cheek. "Carmichael, you have no idea. It hurt so much when you said that. I want to believe you, but my heart... I think you fractured it. I want to tell you I love you."

"You already did when you came to."

The heat of a flush suffused her. "You knew? You heard?" She squirmed in his arms. His chest rumbled with laughter which slowly died away to be replaced with naked hunger.

"Yeah, but right now, I want to show you. Will you let me?"

"Hurry up, cowboy."

He laughed and scooped her up, making for the bed. "You don't need this anymore." He hauled the towel away as his wicked mouth came closer. His eyes, blue and limitless, blazed.

Kumi choked out a brief sentence. "What about the door?"

"Door lock on my command." Then his lips were against hers, moving and mobile as they devoured her.

Her hands were already working at the buttons of his shirt. In short order , she'd bared his glorious broad chest for her. Her fingertips traced the lines and corded muscles of his chest.

With a grunt, he pulled back. "I don't want to hurt you. Your head..."

"Stop now and I'm sure I'm going to die. I'm burning for you, Carmichael. Love me."

He tore at the buttons and clips of his pants and he toed out of his shoes while she shuddered with need. When he returned, there was both hunger and gentleness in his caresses. His hands toyed with her breasts while the heat between her legs left her a melting puddle of wantonness.

His lips found the turgid peaks of her nipples, suckling strongly, and she bowed off the bed, crying out with incomprehensible exhortations. The hairs of his arms rasped over her sensitized skin, arousing her to fever pitch.

Then he pulled back. "I want to pleasure you."

"Together. This time we learn together. We'll have plenty of time for the pleasuring later." She lifted her hand to his head and tugged him down to her. He moved between her legs and she opened to him, giving him access. "I need you, Carmichael. I've never wanted anyone like this."

He fitted himself against her then slowly, with such tenderness, he filled her.

She swallowed the cry that rose in her throat as he stopped, fully seated within her flesh.

She felt so full. *He's mine!* It was the cry of her heart and she held it deep within herself.

"I love you, Kumi."

He nudged, flexing his hips, but her breath caught. He nudged again and she moved against him. Kumi's fingertips grasped his upper arms, urging him on. They moved together, each movement slow and measured.

"Give me everything, Carmichael. Let me feel your need."

He laughed and the sound filled her with joy.

The pace turned wild as they strained and undulated against the other, hurtling toward the ultimate release. The bubble of pleasure grew deep within her gut, spreading out so every inch of her body tingled and shook.

"Car-Carmichael." The sound tore from her throat, and he pounded faster.

The orgasm smashed into her, and she cried out. He gripped her hips as he stilled, as she felt the shooting of seed. The sensation filled her with warmth and heat. She smiled as she closed her eyes.

"Mine. Forever mine," she heard Carmichael say as she let go of reality.

***

Carmichael stretched, Kumi's small body nestled close against him, and smiled. He ran his fingers through the warm silk of her hair, amazed that after every wrong turn, she was still prepared to take a chance with him.

"I feel damned good." He tested the words then started as she began to laugh.

"Do men really say things like that?"

He blushed. "I can't comment about other men."

She reached up and kissed him with a sharp, soul-searing caress. Her pebbled nipples grazed his chest, and he closed his eyes, trying to avoid the flash of arousal that speared him once more.

She toyed playfully with a hair on his chest. "You're so light and I'm so dark."

"Our babies will be beautiful. A mix of you and me."

The words slipped and he heard her gasp. "Babies? You want babies?"

Way to go, opening a can of worms. But when he looked at her, he was entranced.

She smiled, a dreamy, far-away look on her face. "I want babies. I want babies with you."

"I want you too. But we have to catch this madman before it's safe to consider a family."

Her smile was infectious. "I like the sound of that. A family."

"Yeah, me too. But before we can talk about commitment and houses and stuff , we need to find out what my men have found out."

Her smile died away. "Yes, I suppose we do." She swung her legs over the side of the bed, standing up with a gasp. "Darn, I'd forgotten about the headache."

He scanned her through narrowed eyes. "Maybe you should stay here."

"No way. This is about me, so you aren't going to lock me out of the discussions." He held out his hand and she took it, stealing his thoughts. "I think I'm going to need my clothes though."

He looked down at the pile of rumpled underwear and uniform before grabbing them up. "I have a thing for a woman in uniform."

"I'll bet. Now move your backside, mister." She snatched the clothes from his hands and started to pull them on.

Once they were finally dressed, he gripped her hand in his, feeling the rush of pleasure. "Now that you are mine, I want everyone to know. "

Carmichael tugged her along the corridor. Within minutes, they stood outside the tactical offices, watching as the door opened.

Major Bortheays waited, sitting at attention. He quirked an eyebrow at the sight of the two of them. His gaze settled on their entwined hands, but he remained silent as they took seats in front of the glass and metal desk.

"Update me, Major."

"We have the blood type and possible match from the DNA sample."

Carmichael leaned forward, and adrenalin started pumping. "Where and who?" His hands fisted. He'd find the person that tried to murder Kumi. He would make sure they paid.

"Well, you see, that is where the problem exists. Her name is Gillian Edgemont. She's—"

"You are kidding, right? Gillian works for my brother." Not only did Kumi sound shocked, her face paled and she pulled away from him. "She'd never do this. Not ever. Your information is wrong."

Carmichael speared the major with a glare. "Check, then double check, because I will not tolerate a mistake."

Kumi turned disbelieving eyes on him. "Carmichael, I honestly think you have the wrong person. It can't possibly be Gillian."

"Kumi, stop. She's in the perfect location. Knows everyone involved. She's——"

She gripped his fingers tightly and squeezed. "She's also in love with my brother and has been for years. She wouldn't have done this. Trust me. I know her."

"I can't trust anyone when your safety is in the balance." He turned back to the major. "Find the woman and bring her in for interrogation. I want this closed down." When he stood, she went with him, but there was a chasm once more between them. One he couldn't breach. Not yet. In a choice between her safety and this woman, there was no option.

He pushed her through the door, the whole time she was still arguing that Gillian couldn't possibly be the assassin. As soon as the door was closed behind them, he silenced her in the time-honored fashion. She moaned through the kiss, her arms twining around his neck while he soaked up the heat and energy that was Kumi. By the time he pulled back, she was breathless and her eyes shone.

"Why did you do that?"

"Because you need to stop and see this from my perspective. She could be a long-term mole. I have experience with that. Remember Selina?"

Kumi cocked her head to the side. "You think she could be undercover?"

He nodded. "It's possible. I don't need to point out that by destroying Reunion's financial stability, they strike at the very heart of the Federation. I can't take risks. Not with you and not with my mission."

Her face now grave, Kumi nodded. "Okay, but if you're wrong, you owe Tomi and Gillian."

"If I'm wrong, that means keeping you locked down for longer. I want you to be free, but right now we have to be sensible and think this whole thing through."

She nodded, and for the first time, he was sure there was a way forward, if only they could gain clear air.

Chapter 4

"I'm coming with you." Kumi stood after Carmichael announced they were heading down to the planet to pick up Gillian.

"You're staying right here, where you're safe." His eyes flashed like pale blue icicles. Anyone else would be frightened when confronted by the tall, blond man. But she wasn't.

"No. You're going into Tomi's office and arresting his PA. I'm still of the opinion that you have the wrong person." She waited, knowing it was a dangerous game she was playing with his emotions. But she knew Tomi was enamored with the red-haired woman. While he might need a nudge to take the step, this was more of a knocking the legs out from under him. Kumi knew he'd need support. Her support.

Carmichael's lips thinned to long, white lines. "You can't accompany me. It's not the way we work." He watched her and the deep awareness of him told her he wasn't impressed with her actions.

She silently made her way to the door.

"Where the hell are you going?" His voice was a dark rumble, and she smiled. He sounded frustrated and disgusted by her silent rebellion. She knew now that he'd give in.

"I'm heading for the shuttle bay so I can go home." She knew exactly what she was saying and doing. If necessary, she would follow through on her words. Kumi was pretty sure he wouldn't allow her to leave like that.

"You're not." He stepped close and took her hand.

Kumi chanced to look back at him. For just a moment, her determination began to slip. She closed her eyes, remembering why this was important. "Either you take me or I go home. Tomi—"

"Fine."

She stopped at his single bitten out word. Examined it. There were no disclaimers. Just that one word. He meant it. He always said what he meant. "Good. Then let's get going. I'd rather have her name cleared quickly."

He punched the communication center button on his desk. "I'll need a tactical vest, low profile, for Madam Kumi." He let go and glowered. "You follow every instruction I give you. I will not..." He broke off with a pithy epithet as she shook her head.

"I'm sorry, Carmichael, but I have to be there."

He turned away, swiping his hand over his face. "Just stay out of the way and safe." For a short while they both waited in silence then he shook his head in frustration. "Let's round up a team and go get her."

He strode through the door and Kumi raced to keep up. Down the long corridor back to the tactical office, where he marched in grim-faced. "I need a team."

The major stood. "They are already being assembled

in the shuttle bay." He turned surprised eyes on Kumi. "She's not... You're not taking her with you?"

Carmichael grunted and Kumi realized that this was extraordinary behavior. For just a moment a pinprick of self-recrimination gnawed at her. She swiped it away. It was too late to regret her actions.

Things moved quickly then as they made their way to the cavernous gray shuttle bay. Waiting for them were the men he'd worked with previously and others she'd never met before.

Kumi marveled at the array of shuttles lined up on the plascrete flooring even as Carmichael, his hand at the small of her back, pushed her into the open craft.

"I'm fine to climb on—"

"Just take a seat. Wait quietly."

She climbed the steps and took the first seat that was empty in a row of two. She didn't have to like his instructions, but she had promised to follow them.

When he dropped into the seat beside her, he held out a vest. "Put this one while I brief the others." The shuttle took off.

She watched with interest as he shared the facts they had, answered their questions, while dimly noting they were already entering the atmosphere of Reunion .

The shuttle landed on the carefully prepared zone at the top of the Federation offices with a gentle kiss. Then Carmichael took her hand and led her down the steps, all the while checking her vest.

A quick brief touch of her cheek and a whispered "stay behind me" told her of his concern. Tears formed in her eyes as she realized the emotional toll having her along on the mission was taking on him.

The doors before them opened, and as one they made

their way to the stairs. Kumi kept her counsel as they clattered down, one flight then another. Finally, at the thirty-second floor they stopped.

Her breath was coming in pants and she noted none of the men around her were wheezing like she was. "This is so not fair."

Carmichael smiled and the corners of his eyes crinkled. "That's okay. You'll be fit enough to match me, one day." The smile faded away. "Stay safe." He moved away to the front of his men and gave a signal. They moved in formation, not a hand or footstep out of place.

The rear men took her arms. "Stay with us. We'll protect you."

The following moments passed in a blur. She had the impressions of Tomi, his eyes wide with shock which then relayed his anger. "You can't take her."

The sight of Gillian, rising at their request. "I haven't done anything. Tomi?"

Kumi watched as Gillian reached for him, but Carmichael inserted himself between them.

"Under section twenty-one of the Federation Statute, you are hereby detained while we make relevant inquiries. You will now accompany us."

Kumi's stomach knotted as she grasped Tomi's hands. "Come with us, Tomi."

He accepted the tug and she followed Carmichael with the restrained Gillian through the door, the phalanx of tactical officers encircling them. This time they made their way up the stairs at a much slower pace.

Tomi struggled against her embrace. "I need to—"

"Tomi, they have to do their job. Let them find out she's not involved. Be there for her. Be her anchor."

His lips formed white lines while his eyes raged at her.

"I'm here for you both," Kumi assured him. "But you have to understand. Carmichael has a job——"

"His mission was to protect you."

Kumi sighed and let her eyes follow his gaze to the woman at in the secured cell of the shuttle. Gillian's red hair was a stark contrast to her bone white features. Kumi could hear her plaintive cries of "I haven't done anything."

"Then you'll give us the answers we need." Carmichael frowned and looked in Kumi's direction. She saw the worry in his eyes.

"Tomi, you need to fasten yourself in."

Kumi watched as Tomi did so, hearing the click of harnesses around her, and nodded in Carmichael's direction once she was sure Tomi was secure. Her lover took the seat next to their prisoner and they lifted off, the gravitational forces pushing them back against their seats.

Gillian sobbed, her skin turning blotchy. "Why? Why did you arrest me?" Carmichael didn't answer and Kumi understood——he wanted a secure location with recording facilities. A place where he had the technology to follow through on any information he might glean.

When they arrived in the brig, Carmichael had his men take Gillian to an interview room. Kumi worried her lip. "Will she be——"

"You can watch from the viewing room." He pulled her into a tiny room with a large window. Tomi followed them, so there was no real privacy. Carmichael brushed his lips over her cheek. "My men are just outside if you need anything."

He moved away, and the swish of moving metal echoed. He stepped through and het door closed behind him.

"You and Carmichael?"

Kumi nodded at Tomi's words. "Yes. Ever since I met him, it's always been him."

"But his age…" Tomi sounded strained, but she ignored it.

"His age is not an issue, for either of us."

Tomi turned away as the door in the other room opened. They watched through the window as Carmichael stalked into the room. "Take a seat , Gillian. We could be here awhile."

"Where's my representation? I haven't done anything." Gillian's voice wobbled, and Kumi wanted to reach out and fold her arms around the woman.

"Your DNA was found at the scene of a shooting."

Gillian froze. "What scene? What shooting? What are you talking about?" She sniffled as she glanced around, true fear clear on her features.

"An attempt was made on Kumi's life yesterday. Someone with a damned good aim used a laser rifle to—"

"Laser rifle? I don't own one. Besides which, even if I did… Well, everyone knows there is a residue that puffs backward."

Carmichael laughed, it was dark and cold. Kumi shook a little in the viewing room. "This is the man you intend to spend the rest of your life with?" Tomi's voice was heavy with anger.

"I do." She didn't look at her brother, just focused on the tableau unfolding in the room beyond.

"Not everyone knows that. Only someone with experience…" Carmichael leaned just a little more forward, invading Gillian's personal space.

"Captain Snow, I know about these things, okay?"

The red-haired woman shrank back a little in her chair as Carmichael loomed over her. "How do you know?"

"I just do."

"Tell me, Gillian. How do you know this?" Carmichael's voice was silky. *Dangerous.*

"My brother is ex-military," she shouted, and Carmichael started, feeling as if all the wind had been knocked from his lungs.

We didn't even know she had a brother. How did that information escape our investigation? Even worse, her brother is ex-military and we still missed this intelligence? Unforgivable. He tensed as cold fury built inside his gut.

"So how does that account for him having the same DNA as you?" Carmichael raked his fingers through his hair.

"We're twins. He's been deep undercover for some time. Something to do with the Indy freighter movements. So when he joined that section of the Federation forces, they had to delete his records from the systems so no one would know. That just left mine." Gillian bowed her head and placed it on her folded arms where they rested on the metal table. "You'd know the drill better than me. But he's not even here, on planet. Not right now. He had some work to attend to on Ripen 9. He left three days ago."

"Damn it." He turned in the direction of the large window, knowing Kumi was there with her brother Tomi, watching the goings on in the room.

Gillian's words were believable, and he was fairly sure she spoke the truth. He believed her. He knew how the covert forces worked. Hell, he'd written some of the manuals himself.

That didn't mean his people wouldn't make the necessary checks.

As he turned back, he critically scanned her body language. Her stiff posture indicated fear and anger as well as innocence. *Gods, I hope so.* As it was, he was already worried about the fallout from Kumi, not to mention Tomi, after this mission was over.

They needed information, as much as they could get.

"Fine. Then you won't have any problems giving us his address and those he is known to associate with."

She started, lifting her head. The black liner around her eyes had run and he noted the rivulets of black trailing down her face. "Yeah. Sure. But can you...you know, release me for a moment so I can wipe my face?"

Carmichael released her restraints, giving into his well-honed instincts. She smiled —a wobble of her lips—as she accepted the tissues then swiped away the black from her cheeks. "It's a good thing the senator can't see me. He likes his staff to look immaculate at all times."

Frowning at her words, Carmichael was left feeling like something scraped off the bottom of a shoe. *Just how much damage have I done if she is innocent?*

He shrugged the thought away. Kumi had to be safe, so she could save the planet from financial ruin, and so they could be together. Kumi or Gillian? There was no contest in his mind.

Even as he watched Gillian finger-comb her hair, he pulled out his scribe pad and noted down the information she gave him. The list wasn't long, but he was sure it was pretty close to exhaustive.

Gillian laid her head on the table as Carmichael headed for the door. It slammed shut behind him and his long strides took him to the viewing room where Kumi waited with her brother.

This time Carmichael wasn't taking any chances. He'd leave her there on the ship where she could be protected. If the bastard was on Reunion, he'd find him.

At the door to the viewing room he stopped. *I could just leave. Not tell her.* For an instant, he toyed with the thought. It would stop her machinations, but reality impinged. That might damage their relationship, his mind countered. So he discounted the idea. The door opened at his command and Kumi was there. Waiting for him.

"I know. You have to go. This time I won't..." She launched herself at him, her lips whispering against his neck. For a moment, he savored the feel of her, close against him. "Just come back to me safe, okay?"

His chest expanded with pride while he thanked his stars that this woman was his. He pulled away. "Hopefully this won't take long." Then he turned and left her.

Waiting for Carmichael to return felt like the longest hours of her life. The *Emancipation's* men showed her to the galley and she thanked them for the kindness. She decided to grab a cup of tea, hoping it would occupy her hands and mind while she waited. Tomi followed her and gave instructions that Gillian also have her needs attended to.

Once they sat down though, Tomi barely spoke and her heart bled for him. She had experienced the pain of thinking Carmichael hadn't wanted her, how much worse was his? He'd pushed Gillian aside and now had to watch as she was arrested and interrogated , considered a suspect in his sister's attempted assassination.

"Tomi, you know he was just going his job, don't you?"

He turned away with a grunt and she sighed against the lip of her cup. It would take time to heal this wound. So she sipped at the hot tea in her hands.

When the medic appeared just over Tomi's shoulder she smiled. "I'm fine, you know." Her smile died away when she noted the look on his face. Black oily sensations crept up her spine. Cold seeped into her pores.

"No. Madam Kumi..."

"Carmichael. He's hurt."

The medic nodded, and her heart rate slowed.

"He's..." She couldn't finish the thought. *He promised to come back in one piece* . "I have to..." She jerked up, the tea spilling.

Tomi was there, his hand holding hers, standing beside her. She didn't know how he got there. Didn't care. Right now she needed her brother.

"Is he here yet?" She wanted to move, but didn't know where to go. Her brain wouldn't function. *Carmichael!* She wanted to scream her frustration and fear.

"Madam Kumi, we don't yet know the extent of his injuries , but the team has him enroute."

"Where? Where will they take him?" The medic looked startled at her demand. "What? Oh...the shuttle bay. They'll enter via the shuttle bay."

She surged forward, dragging Tomi after her. They arrived in the cavernous hangar as the gray craft landed on the plascrete in silence, while her heart beat rapidly, somewhere in the region of her throat.

"Gods, don't let him be hurt badly. Please."

Tomi squeezed her fingers, and she drew strength from his as she focused on the transport.

The door opened with a loud hiss. The first sound she heard was him growling at his men. "This is ridiculous and overkill. It's only a flesh wound."

Her breath whooshed out. Assured he wasn't dead or on death's door, her knees wobbled as if they'd collapse beneath her. She straightened her spine as he appeared at the aperture and noted the dark patch at his shoulder, the charred edges of his uniform. Her stomach roiled.

Kumi rushed forward, stopping in front of him.

Carmichael's eyes narrowed and she saw the banked anger in his gaze, swallowed her worry and barked, "You get that seen to before you interrogate anyone, Captain. And that's an order."

The men around him laughed before smothering their outburst with coughs. "I need to get the information..." But his words died away. "Fine."

He turned to his men, hissing as the movement must have pulled on the wound site. "Take him through to Interrogation Two. Make sure there is no contact with the other prisoner."

His men hauled the suspect between them. He sported a bloodied nose and grazed cheek while groaning and shuffling along. She couldn't regret any action they'd taken, because it meant she had Carmichael there with her. Maybe not whole and hale, but alive and spitting, and that was fine with her.

Once Carmichael had been attended to, he insisted on interrogating the man, Anderson Edgemont. Gillian's brother, Kumi had to remind herself. She sat in the viewing room appraising him. His red hair was paler than Gillian's long, bright locks and his chin was weak. His eyes seemed shifty in Kumi's mind.

"State your full name for the record." Carmichael in action was a sight to see. He lounged indolently against the wall, an almost bored expression on his face. Kumi knew the looks were deceiving. A muscle in his hand jumped and jerked.

"I don't have to." Anderson moved restlessly in his chair with a smug expression.

"Hmm, maybe, maybe not. My men found traces of laser residue on your clothing." Carmichael pushed away from the wall, his lope restrained and yet somehow animal-istic. Slowly, he advanced on the prisoner, stopping mere inches away and leaning down. "But maybe you're just a good lad." With the flat of his hand, he slapped the man on his left shoulder.

Anderson jumped with a yelp. "You can't do this. It's intimidation."

The smile that crept over Carmichael's face was feral. "This is a military inquiry. You know what that means."

The man paled. Normal interrogation rules were suspended in situations where military statutes were enabled.

"You can't be serious. I'm just—" Then he stopped and slumped back into his chair. "Representation. I want a rep."

"What a shame, there isn't any here. Just you and me." Carmichael leaned in closer. "Who's your contact? Who are you working for Anderson Edge-mont? Who is so important your only sister's life is on the line?"

Now the man gulped and Kumi felt the coiled snakes in her belly twist.

"He won't turn Gillian into a bargaining chip." Tomi spoke, his tones furious . Kumi laid a soft hand on his arm.

"He won't. Trust me. He doesn't harm innocents. I'm sure of that." Tomi pulled away from her touch. "Just let him do what he has to."

"Damn it. Damn you, she's not involved," Anderson yelled, and Kumi's gaze flicked back to the room beyond. "She's got nothing to do with it."

"Then you'll tell me who and I can let her go. Otherwise..." Carmichael waited as the man tugged on his bonds. Letting him draw his own conclusions.

"Dobry. Dobry Tichenko. In Madam Kumi's office. He's the contact with the Indy warriors."

This time it was her turn to feel shock. *Dobry?* He was the traitor?

The night drew in while Carmichael settled Kumi in his cabin, unwilling to let her go. Keeping her close meant he could protect her .

"Will you?" She indicated the bed.

He shook his head. "No. I need to do this first."

She nodded and lay down, a hiss escaping, reminding him she wasn't anywhere near healed.

Carmichael settled himself on the chair in front of the computer screen. Turning his mind to the case, he wanted to snarl. The man, Dobry, was a sleaze. That much had been obvious in the way he'd oozed in Kumi's presence. But on top of that, he was willing to watch her die. To order her death while pretending he wanted some kind of a relationship with her.

"Over my dead body."

"Carmichael? Did you say something?" She lifted her head with a wince and his fury ratcheted up yet another notch.

The thought of the man's cold-blooded planning fueled the rage that he'd banked deep inside him. The light pen in his hand snapped with a crack. Tiny dribbles of blood ran over his fingers. Only two questions remained in his mind—why and how.

Seeking the evidence he needed was only way to end the man's schemes. But there were so many levels of security in the system when dealing with the global government. Each search string needed an administrator override. He swore his frustration as the machine in front of him beeped.

"Perhaps I can help you?" He turned at Kumi's soft words. She'd slid off the bed and made her way over while he'd cussed. The fact was he couldn't access the information. They needed help.

"I can't get into the secure human resources server."

Kumi rounded the desk, and for one moment, he was tempted to pull her down to his lap. To kiss her. His body reacted, turning hard, but he noted the shadowed eyes and the tight lines around her mouth. He damned his libido and moved aside to give her access to the screen.

Kumi worked at the keyboard. "You know, I would never have guessed Dobry was behind this. I thought he was my friend."

He rubbed her shoulder as she sighed. It was long and sad sounding. "How long have you known him?" He watched with interest as she tapped in the override sequence.

The machine flashed and beeped. *Permission Denied.*

"What the... Why is it saying permission denied?" She

started again, whispering her actions as the keyboard clacked. Again, the machine flashed the same message. "Gillian is a whiz with this stuff. Let me get her." She stilled and looked in his direction, having half risen from her chair.

"I'd rather not. She's…"

"She's not just a PA. She is also a trained comp tech."

Thoughts skittered through his mind. The one that stood out was that he needed help.

They had to find Dobry and his background before he took flight. *If we lose him…*

"Do it."

Kumi depressed the communicator, found the cabin that Gillian had been moved to, and arranged an escort. "We can trust her. I know we can."

Carmichael kept his own concerns under wraps. When the ding of the door let them know that Gillian had arrived, he was calm and controlled. On the outside, anyway. His men had apprised him that Tomi had followed Gillian into the tiny space of the cabin earlier. While he wanted to ask what was said, he kept his mouth shut. It wasn't his business.

Kumi quickly explained the situation, and Gillian took up a seat, tapping on the keys with brutal efficiency. The first time the permission denied screen flashed he felt a surge of satisfaction. She'd been as stymied as them. But when he glanced at Gillian, she was smiling. "Oh, clever bugger, aren't you?"

Again, the woman tapped commands, but this time a yellow screen flashed. "Usually when techs create a system like this, they chatter about their work. I'd heard some whispers that a back door entry was left open."

They entered the main system. "Find me everything on Dobry Tichenko."

Gillian nodded. "You know, if I was a bad guy, I'd probably be able to fudge this and you and your techs would never know."

The thought had already crossed Carmichael's mind. That and how could he head hunt her for his crew if she was truly innocent. The sound of the door opening split his attention for a moment, and Tomi entered the cabin. Carmichael's face tightened, and he found it odd that Kumi's brother would be there now. "What made you come here?"

Tomi's lips thinned. "One of the men alerted me that Gillian was here. What are you—"

"Hang on. What's this?" Gillian's tense voice broke Carmichael's concentration for an instant.

There, on the screen, was a tiny blip, and they all focused on it. Four heads leaned close to the computer.

"He's been amending the system. Let me find his override passcode." Gillian tapped, but it beeped.

Another screen opened. A smiling face with text below.

Kumi read the words on the screen. *"You've been beaten by Danyr Gubanovski.* Who the hell is that?"

But Carmichael knew of Danyr Gubanovski. He'd been a fighter for the Indy's. A force to be reckoned with. He'd disappeared. "Check the records. I need an address, the date he started, and his position."

It was starting to come together.

"Dobry lives in the hinterlands. Close to Vesparia. He's been in the department for eight years. I have his address."

Gillian's information helped him to make up his mind. He watched the tiny printout emerging from the slot and snatched it up. He needed a team tonight. Now. Before it was too late.

"That was before I started. Not long before the credits started to run out." Kumi's voice was dry. "It was all there, all the time. I'll bet Nordric, my predecessor, had no idea of what was going on. Just look at the way he's managed to manipulate the HR systems."

Carmichael felt the coiling of tension inside his gut. "Tomi, I need you to stay here with the women. I'm rounding up a team."

"But you're hurt! You shouldn't be..." Kumi subsided as he shot her a look. "Fine. Just don't get hurt again."

He leaned in, dropping a quick, hard kiss on her lips. "Sleep, and I'll be back before you know it." He moved with speed, pressing his communicator while he shot rapid fire commands to his team. By the time he arrived in the shuttle bay, they were assembled and ready to go.

The shuttle slipped out of the bay and into the darkness of space as the planet of Reunion loomed large. As the ship hurtled toward the surface, he outlined the plan. "We go in quick. Unless he has some kind of alert on the systems, he won't know we're on our way. I want him alive if possible. The information he has access to could help us solve this whole Indy guerrilla cell."

They nodded and as the land rose, they tugged on tactical vests. His communications officer broke off discussions with the local guards. "They'll stay out of the way."

Carmichael indicated that he'd heard.

One by one, his men clambered out of the shuttle and formed up. *They're a damned fine team. I've been proud to command them, but for the first time in a long while, I know there is more in my future.*

A light shone in the window ahead. Not far away an

Indy lay, likely sleeping, probably dreaming of overthrowing the Federation. A grin settled on Carmichael's face. "Never. The Federation will never fall. Not on my watch."

In the dark night, his men moved, flowing toward their target, the clicks of comm badges letting him know they were ready. He counted... *Ten, eleven, twelve. Everyone in place.*

"Naval Investigations! Hit the floor and await instructions!" The cry filled the night air as they shoved through locked doors like a knife through melted butter.

Calls of "clear" filled the night until one voice shouted out, "Captain! You better come here."

In a small back room lay the body of Dobry. A beeping alarm sounded softly in the distance.

"Gods damn it. Too damned late." Kumi stretched, feeling the post-sex glow, and waited in silence. Carmichael wanted to talk, she could tell. He'd only been back under an hour , but she'd needed assurance that this time he was back without any further injuries. One thing led to another... She grinned again.

He'd been gone longer than planned, collecting the information that would lead them to whoever was in charge of the Indies. She knew he hadn't taken Dobry into custody, but they'd found information and leads. Things that would help them find the heart of the threat to the Federation.

"I'm getting too old to keep this up. I'm slowing down." His drowsy voice filled the air. "You're what? Forty-nine? That's hardly old." She smiled, rubbing her hand up and down his naked bicep.

"For a combat officer it is. Besides, now that I have you , I want to come home every night. I want to watch you get big and fat. I don't want to miss out on watching our babies grow."

Her movements stopped. "What's brought this on, Carmichael? Something has bothered you since you returned from searching Dobry's home." Kumi levered herself so she lay against the pillows.

"I remember that area. I grew up on Reunion. One of the small farming villages nearby. I used to think nothing ever happened here. That Reunion was somehow the back end of the Federation. It's why I joined the Naval forces. I promised myself I didn't want a family. No ties. That was the life I craved."

"You grew up on Reunion? I would never have guessed," she teased, but he grimaced, scratching slightly at his chest. The bared expanse dried her mouth, leaving her hungry for more. It was scarred and battle-worn, but that was Carmichael. *My man.*

"I want to do the whole thing with you, Kumi. I know I'm a lot older, but I want to spend the rest of my life with you. I want to be the man standing beside you. Will you make your commitment to me?"

It was the question she'd wanted to hear from him since the day they'd met at Selina and Renjiro's ceremony. Her heart did a slow pound in her chest. "Yes, Carmichael, I will."

"Good. Now let's start on that first baby." He rolled her over, setting his lips against hers , and her last thought was that she'd finally found her forever.

PART III

Executing Justice

The end game is looming, but whether the last of the Ito family will find his happily ever after is in the balance.

Tomi Ito must deal with the knowledge that the woman he's loved forever, Gillian Edgemont, thinks he's abandoned her in her time of need. But when he's abducted, she's there to help save him.

Gillian is running from the wreck of her life and the unrequited passion she holds for her former boss, Senator Tomi Ito. When he follows her to Vega II so does the danger that's been dogging the Ito family.

As the finale looms, does it include a future for Tomi and Gillian? Or will it all turn to ashes?

Chapter 1

Gillian sighed heavily as she leaned her aching head against the bolster. No matter how many different ways she tried to see her brother's—her twin's—choices, there was never anything that made them seem any better. But then, how could it? Her twin, Anderson, had organized a hit on the sister of the man Gillian loved.

"How could you do this?" In the darkness, there was no answer.

She rubbed her brow. Her life was in tatters, just as his was. Her position as the personal assistant to Senator Ito had disappeared like fog on a summer morning, thanks to Anderson's stupid actions. With a conviction against his name, she couldn't access any of the highly confidential information that came with her job. She was now deemed a ' security risk'.

As a result, she'd been dismissed by a chair jockey from the Central Registry of Employment. The CRE oversaw all positions within the government. She didn't like it. Not one bit. All the years she'd worked tirelessly had been dissolved in one pen stroke. But there was no avenue of appeal. *So much for natural justice.*

"Ugh, why couldn't you have done something else, like…be a baker? Damn it, Anderson." She dragged the pillow over her face to muffle the sound of the words her mother shouldn't hear and to absorb her angry tears. She already had enough to be concerned about, with her only son in the prison system now and her daughter unable to secure a job.

"Gillian, dear? Is everything okay?" The querulous sound of her mother's voice from the next bedroom had her sitting up and sighing.

"Yeah, everything is fine, Ma. You go to sleep."

Gillian listened for the rustling sound of her mother settling in her bed. The worst part was that she missed her boss. The job had been great, acting as his executive assistant had brought with it a range of experiences. But it was the time spent in his company that had given her the most satisfaction and fulfillment. Tomi. If she closed her eyes, she could see him in her mind. Toned and golden brown, with a hint of the orient in the slant of his eyes.

She huffed in the silence. "Now there'll be no more of that." With the thought came a pang of loss. Another salty tear traced its way down her face. She brushed it away. "No use in crying over what can never be." But between Anderson's actions and Tomi's lack of contact, her life felt like little more than a pile of ashes .The introspection didn't stop the pain that wracked her system. Glancing out the window, she could see the moon high in the sky.

"I wonder if he is looking at the same moon and wondering about me ." Gillian cursed herself for her foolish thoughts before slumping back into the bedcovers.

She dragged the pillow under her head and turned

away from the window. *I should get some sleep. Tomorrow I'll need to look for work.* Her heart still ached as she closed her eyes and let sleep claim her.

Tomi tossed and turned, angry with himself and the rules the CRE had enacted. It didn't matter that he'd voted for them with the very best of intentions, because this time, he knew they were causing pain to an innocent person. Right now, somewhere out there, Gillian probably thought no one would employ her because of her brother's conviction. And she was probably right. Reunion was such an insular planet that it was likely a correct assumption. But he couldn't do a damned thing about it.

In his mind, the replay of the scene from earlier in the day ran like an old-fashioned video.

"Senator Ito? This is Cyrelle from the Central Registry. The brother of your executive assistant, Gillian Edgemont, has been found guilty of a second level treason offence. As such, Miss Edgemont must now be considered a security risk. We plan to terminate her employment in your office, effective immediately."

Whoever this Cyrelle was, she was brisk and businesslike while making the announcement. Shock stole his breath. What the…
"What? You can't."

"I'm sorry, Senator. These are the rules that were implemented by the senate. You can, of course, appeal, but her employment must be terminated at this time."

He dropped his forehead into his hands, knowing that there was no mistake. The woman was right. Gillian's brother had conspired with an Indy assassin to kill his sister, Kumi. It meant Gillian was tainted by association, even though that was an unwarranted tag. But it still stank like three-day-old oysters.

In this instance, he should be the one to handle it he told himself. "Let me——"

"No, Senator. We have found it's best if we handle the process. It makes it easier on all involved. I'll send someone up to collect her things, if you could arrange for a staffer to clear her personal items. All passwords and authorities which are held by the Central Registry are being suspended immediately. If she has any personal authorizations in your office, please don't hesitate to inform us, and we will handle the situation as a priority." Her voice was soft, understanding even, but it ripped his guts out to hear Gillian's life being dismantled in such a bloodless manner.

"Will she..." He paused, struggling with himself to finish the question, but before he could proceed the woman spoke again..

"We will offer her as much assistance as possible, but at the end of the day, we must make full disclosure as to her termination should it be requested."

"Yes, I understand." Even as he agreed, his heart roared at the unfairness of the situation.

Now he lay in the dark, his stomach churning. "There must be something I can do." He checked the chrono on his wrist, but it was only two in the morning and he couldn't make contact with anyone. Instead, he was forced to relive every time he'd let Gillian down. The instances seemed numerous.

Looking back, he considered that circumstances of their meeting had been fated. His elevation had been unplanned. Things had been tough on Reunion as battle-weary soldiers returned, many shattered by their experiences in the war. His cousin, Renjiro, had come home and immediately accepted a position with the Justice Department. Ren had been unable to even conceive of a position in authority at that point. He'd been wired and jittery, and Tomi had the impression he'd chosen to use it to search for something amorphous. But now they all knew why. He'd been searching for his lover, Selina.

Tomi's uncle gave him the chance to take the seat that should have been Renjiro's. His uncle had been an understanding man, and there'd been a tacit agreement that if at some point Ren decided he wanted to join the senate, then Tomi would help him achieve that.

Tomi had first met Gillian when he was a fresh senator, and she'd been working for another. He'd watched her from a distance for many long months, and when his uncle's assistant decided to move on, the opportunity to grab Gillian for his staff seemed like fate.

Gillian had been a godsend, quiet and efficient in every way that counted. If he was honest, she was partly responsible for his meteoric rise through the senate to become the leader. Most people only saw her bubbly surface, but she had a capable head on her shoulders and a loyalty that had made her an asset. Gillian had moved into the office with smooth capability, taken it in hand, and streamlined the systems. He'd been captivated by her fiery red hair and green eyes. Yet, she'd never shown a scrap of interest in him.

The only time was… He wrenched his thoughts away. That would only lead to more issues and self-recrimination. Instead, he thrust back the covers and rose. Tomi padded across the room, his nude body limned by the moonlight.

"Perhaps an hour in the gym will let help me clear these thoughts." He reached for the light exercise clothing he'd thrown on the dressing chair earlier and tugged them over his body.

Stalking in the direction of his gym, towel flung across his shoulder, he didn't notice the person shadowing him until it was too late. A re-breather covered his mouth and nose. His hands tore at the fleshy fingers holding the mask in place, his years of training abandoning him in the moment. The gas overtook his senses and he dropped like a stone to the floor. As the last vestiges of consciousness ebbed away, he depressed the button on his chrono, hoping someone would find him.

*B*ang! The sound woke Gillian with a jerk. "Who… Huh?" She tumbled from the bed, the sheets tangled around her legs. Another bang reverberated.

"Open for the Justice Department!" a voice roared through the closed front door, and Gillian shook the last strands of sleep from her mind as she struggled out of the linen restraints.

Justice Department? What could they possibly want?

"I'm coming!" As she made for the door, clutching her robe to her chest, she noted her mother, frozen with a look of horror on her face, but there was no time to settle her fears. "It's okay, Ma. I'll find out what they want and they'll go away." She hoped it would be that easy, anyway.

A rattle came at the door as Gillian thrust her arms into the robe with a jerk.

"I'm coming," she called again, hoping they wouldn't bash down the door. But they rattled and shook it again. For a moment, she was sure the door surviving intact was a vain hope. She grasped the handle and pulled, opening it inward.

On the other side stood a small knot of men dressed in black combat suits. They hovered, their faces hard as they watched her. The weak light shone on the rubberized fabric, making them look almost wet.

"Gillian Edgemont? We have a warrant to search for Senator Tomi Ito." The man who spoke brusquely brushed past her and entered her house.

"I am, yes. And you're here because ..." She waited, assuming what she hoped was a confident pose, even as the shock rocketed through her system. *Well, as confident as you can be in short pajamas and a robe while a troop of men tromped into your house unannounced*, she thought sourly, trying to discount their words. *Looking for Senator Tomi Ito.*

"Captain Elstrath. Here is a warrant allowing us to search these premises." He gave a quick gesture and they flooded in. The piece of paper—*warrant,* her battered mind corrected her—was shoved into her hands.

The man opposite eyed her up and down, his eyes cold and distant, and it felt like being touched by a dirty rag. The resultant response of her body was to shiver with distaste. It took a lot of effort to control her reaction.

"You are known to conspire with traitors and your past association with Senator Ito led us here. If you know anything about his disappearance..."

Gillian's heart stuttered in her chest. "What do you mean his disappearance?" She looked around wildly as the men started turning over cushions and opening draws and doors. It would never have occurred to her that something might happen to him. *Where were his minders?* She glanced around and saw others similarly going through her things.

"What are you doing?" The spiral of disbelief bloomed deep in her head.

"We have a warrant to search for anything that will give us a clue as to his whereabouts." The words fell like heavy rocks thudding down on her consciousness.

Search? What did they… Then it occurred to her. Her brother was a traitor. "Oh gods!" She pulled up the chair at the square table and slumped into it.

A light touch of a hand drew her attention. "It'll be all right, won't it, Gillian?"

She slid a shaking hand over her mother's and said a silent prayer, asking for forgiveness for the lie she was about to tell. "I hope so, Ma. I bet everything comes to rights before you know it. It might be best if you go home to Dad tomorrow."

"You need me right now."

Gillian wanted to cry, hearing the careful tones of her mother, knowing how much the last few months had cost her emotionally. "I'll be fine. In fact, as soon as I can, I'll come home for a break. I have a few things I need to do first, though."

Her mother moved away then found another chair and pulled it out before she sank down. Around them, people murmured as they lifted cushions and peered around corners. The sense of violation speared Gillian, but she knew there wasn't anything she could do. They were within their rights—the evidence was there on the table in front of her. *Warrant To Search And Seize.*

In the deepest recesses of her mind, she thought over what the big man had told her. Tomi had disappeared. That hurt even more than watching these brutes in her house. She ignored the pain. Now wasn't the time to examine it.

Instead, she watched and waited while they scoured her home, and when they were finally done, she was left with a dirty and defiled sensation.

Her mother insisted on changing the bedding once they'd left, and Gillian simply nodded and pushed the door shut. She rested her head against the wood and sucked in an unsteady breath. Maybe it was time to accept that her life here on Reunion was done. She'd had offers from other senators and senior executive positions before it had all blown up. Well, before her brother had plunged her into this mess. Could she dare hope? But the thought fled. The CRE would have to make full disclosure. Then who would want her?

Even as she grappled with that reality, the communications device beeped. Gillian rushed in its direction, wondering who could be ringing at this hour of the night.

"Gillian? It's Kumi. Can you come here, please?" The broken tones of the diminutive woman—the sister of Tomi —tore at her.

"Oh Kumi, I'm not sure…" Even though Gilian knew Kumi couldn't see her—a fact she was grateful for—she still shook her head.

"Carmichael thinks he might be able to find Tomi, but we need your assistance."

The idea that she might be instrumental in finding Tomi, in saving him, was heady. She sucked in a deep breath. *Gods, perhaps…*

Gillian knew exactly what she had to do. "Okay, give me a few minutes to get dressed and settle Ma, and I'll be on my way." She depressed the button and the call ended. Even as she was striding to the bedroom, she called out, "Ma! I gotta go out and leave you here for a while. Get some sleep!"

Hurling the pajamas onto a pile on the floor, Gillian promised to burn them. After the look that man had given her…

"No. Just get dressed. There are better things to dwell on." She hauled on long, black pants, boots, a loose top, and a black jacket. She was running a brush through her hair when her mother ducked around the door.

"Where are you going?"

"I have some stuff I need to attend to. Lock the door after me and keep your communicator close. I'll be back as soon as I can." Then, after a swift hard hug, she hurried for the door.

An aching pain shot through Tomi's head as consciousness rose. *Don't open your eyes until you know it's safe. Keep your breathing even.* The lessons his security team had tried to instill in him halted his instinctive actions. Tomi embraced them, knowing they might be his only path to freedom.

He expanded his lungs and listened. The more his ears strained, the more creaking and groaning he could hear. The creak and groan of a ship—old and wooden—his helpful mind supplied the fact. Tomi had spent a lot of time on the water as a teenager at his family's beach house, but he was pretty sure he wasn't there. Something about it felt… *It just doesn't feel right.* Tomi nearly snorted at his own thought. Of course it wouldn't. He was trussed up like some game hen!

After a while, when he was sure there was no one around, he opened his eyes bit by painful bit, glancing through eyelashes until finally he was able to see clearly. He was alone, just as he'd hoped.

Better not to speak though, in case they are within earshot. His legs cramped, and he tightened the muscles before releasing them.

His hands brushed against a wood floor, old and rough. A splinter slid beneath the surface of the soft pad of his fingers. He hissed and tugged, but his hands were tightly bound. Tied hand and foot. Whoever they were, and whatever they intended to do, it didn't include him escaping easily. Too bad he had no intentions of falling in with their plans.

The edge of his chrono snagged on the bindings and he smiled. "Yeah." He only breathed the words then looked quickly in the direction of the door he'd noted earlier. No movement. So they hadn't yet detected that he'd woken.

Bending his legs, he studied the bindings. Pre-Indy War wrist restraints. He smiled. They would be old and maybe brittle. With that in mind, Tomi slowly began rubbing his legs up and down in opposite directions and was quickly rewarded with a twang as they gave. *One more thing in my favor.* If only he could get his hands free. The more he tugged and pulled though, the less agile his hands became. By the end, they felt swollen and useless.

Another quick glance around the room didn't immediately offer any solutions to his problem, so he slumped onto the unforgiving surface.

A sound caught his attention and he glanced up in time to see the door creak open.

A female, slight and cautious, slipped into the cell. "I brung you a drink, mister." Her voice rasped, and the raging thirst he'd ignored grew.

"Thank you." He watched, noting the matting hanks of hair, dirty space coverall, and bare feet. He couldn't see her face, but he could smell the waft of stale sweat and sex that emanated from her. His gag reflex pulsed and he swallowed hard. She stiffened for an instant, before whatever emotion melted away.

She bobbed her head and came closer. "You done freed your feet. Master won't be happy."

"Where am I?"

The girl, he was sure she wasn't very old, held out a cup with a straw, and he ignored any concerns of what might be on it, drawing deeply. Water, cool and fresh, slid down the back of his throat, and he felt his body relaxing.

When she tugged the cup away, he sighed. "Thank you."

Her startled gaze turned his stomach. No one probably thanked her for anything, he realized.

"You be on a boat." As if she'd done something wrong, she whipped around. "I gotta go." Then she hurried like a scared rabbit back through the heavy door. It thudded closed and he heard the grating turn of a lock.

Master. She called whoever she was scared of that and it made Tomi feel ill. The man was obviously using her in every way possible. Tomi promised himself that at the end of this ordeal, when he was saved, he'd take her with him. Offer her sanctuary and help. Find her family.

"You need to get out before you can help her." He muttered the words, willing himself to try again. Heavy thuds and a cry filled the air and he looked up, startled, but no one came. Then it was silent again.

Rain fell. The air outside turned cool and puffs of steam rose from her mouth as Gillian jogged to her car. After tonight, she was more wary than ever, and she glanced around as if she expected one of the searchers from earlier to emerge from the darkness.

Under the solar-generated lamps, her vulnerability slammed home. There she was, on her own, with no one person she could call on for help. As Gillian waved the data key over the sensor, the door unlocked and she slumped into the vehicle seat with a grateful sigh. A touch of the ignition and a simple request for destination were attended to and she waited as the late model air-car rose in the sky.

"Let him be safe." As expected, there was no response.

She traveled several miles before the car made a quiet and efficient landing on a well-guarded street. She'd never been here before, though Tomi had offered on more than one occasion for her to 'tag along' as he called it. Because of the depth of her feelings for him, it had always seemed wise to avoid those kinds of social and personal interactions. There had been no use in dreaming of what she couldn't have, she'd reasoned. Now she damned herself for her foolish scruples.

As Gillian climbed from the small vehicle, a light shone on her. "Who are you? State your business." A young man in a tidy military uniform of gray-blue stepped forward.

She squinted in the strong light, feeling at a disadvantage. "Madam Kumi contacted me. My name is Gillian."

Before she could finish her answer, he stepped back and away. "Ah yes, Madam Kumi informed me that we should expect you. Come this way." The officer executed a perfect military one-hundred-and-eighty-degree turn on his heel with a squeak before he marched out of the light.

Gillian followed him toward a metal entry hidden behind lush shrubbery. The gate swung open in silence and beyond it she saw the silhouette of a house, a single light flickering in a window.

The guard crunched up the path and she shadowed him, feeling insignificant and out of place. He stopped at the door, gave two precise raps then stepped back.

The door flung open. "Gillian! I'm so pleased you're here." The whirlwind that was Kumi flung her arms around Gillian's shoulder, pulling her close. "We need your help."

Urgent hands tugged her inside and Gillian heard the thud of a door closing at her back, but kept her eyes forward. The entrance was large but comfortable, paneled in dark wood and bronze. Kumi pulled her into another white painted room. Overstuffed couches—real antiques, Gillian was sure—vied for space among technical gadgetry, but the effect seemed right. In the corner waited a man. He was more like a hulking mountain, but Gillian knew him. He was Carmichael Snow, husband to Kumi Ito.

Gillian stopped, unable to proceed. The last time she'd seen him was at her brother's sentencing. She didn't like the man all that much, not after he'd dragged her from Tomi's office like a criminal.

"Miss Edgemont, I'm pleased you're here." His voice boomed and she started.

"Really? I doubt that, Captain. After all, you arrested me, removed me forcibly from my office. Arrested my brother…" She stopped and drew an unsteady breath. Her hand rose unconsciously to her throat.

"I was doing my job." He shrugged.

She supposed he was, but it wasn't something she could accept lightly. He'd humiliated her and now, because of his actions, her brother was incarcerated on a moon base and she was unemployable.

"Carmichael? Gillian? Come sit down and we can discuss the problem." Kumi moved gracefully to the seats and lowered herself into a deep chair.

Once again, Gillian was filled with the sense of unreality. She followed Kumi's example though and sank into the comfortable cushions. "So what do you need from me?" Gillian kept her gaze on Carmichael as she waited for his answer.

He shifted behind her and she craned, looking to see him pick up a small, hand based unit. "Tomi was taken from his home. He only had time to set the emergency distress button on his chrono. But they are using some kind of a blocker. We can't trace him. I need—we need you to initiate a bounce-back sequence that will allow us to override the blocking. Kumi says you have extraordinary computation skills, which I've seen before. But this is different. Can you do it?"

Thinking fast, she nodded. "Depending on what kind of program his chrono device is using, I might be able to. Do you have—" The tablet was thrust into her hands and she sighed. "Okay, let me take a look."

Slowly, she traced her hands over the initial transmission. *A Chrono-Desi-Five... Hard to hack, good quality.* She'd known someone working for the company years ago, during her final years at college, and he was always yapping about the tiny glitch in the coding he'd been working on.

"I can break this."

Her fingers flew over the screen, tracking the entry sequence and entering the override password he'd once let slip. Every now and again, a failsafe message would flicker on the screen. The security features of the chrono were extensive. It took several hours to make her way through the layers of security. The sun rose as she huddled over the device. At some point, a drink was thrust into her hands and she gratefully gulped it down.

The touch of gentle fingers and a quiet, "Take a break," broke her concentration momentarily. She looked up to see concern on Kumi's face .

"I'm nearly there. All I have to do is—"

"You've been at it for seven hours. You need a break. If you make a mistake because you're tired, it won't help Tomi." Then Kumi bit her lip, her eyes turning watery.

Carmichael drew Kumi close and Gillian turned away, feeling like a voyeur at the intimate embrace. "We'll find him, Kumi. If Gillian can find and break the override command, access the repeating code…"

Gillian's heart sank at the question in his voice. Carmichael didn't believe she could do it. Angry with him and herself, she dragged the screen close again and scrutinized the code. "There you are." She breathed the words and smiled. She'd found the repeating code and the link to his chrono embedded within it.

Chapter 2

The seep of cold into Tomi's bones was causing him issues. His bladder was full to bursting and his teeth chattered. *It wasn't so bad before, but now...* Tomi huddled on the floor, wishing for a bathroom, a blanket, and rescue.

It had been hours since the girl had brought him a drink. Hours when wherever he was had been as silent as a grave and he felt a pang of fear for the girl. Then a sliver of light had appeared and he'd breathed deeply.

Now, after all these long hours, a creak warned him that someone was about to enter. Was it the mysterious *Master*, the girl, or someone else?

It was the girl again, but this time she was unsteady on her feet.

"Are you okay?" He leaned forward and grimaced as an arc of pain seared his shoulders. She flinched away and his stomach roiled. "Master says you need to pee." She stretched out her arm, covered in the grimy coverall. In her hand was a bucket. He looked at it, revolted by the thought he'd have to relieve himself in front of her. "You stand, I'll help."

"I'd rather…" The thought of doing something so intimate in front of her was more than an indignity. It stripped away the layers of civilization. Why were they doing this? And why to him? The thought he'd been grappling with since waking still had no answer .

She shrank back. "Master says bucket." Then she pressed the receptacle in his direction again.

Tomi needed to go urgently and this might be his only chance for some time. He bit back the sounds of discomfort as he pushed his feet beneath himself. The girl lids a hand under his armpit and hauled. He wobbled uncertainly to his feet, focused on a point ahead of himself while the girl helped him to attend to business. When it was done, he slumped back to the floor, feeling somehow less human.

"Why am I here?"

He noted the way the girl stilled. "Master says not to talk." She collected the bucket and made for the door before stopping. She glanced in the direction of the heavy barrier then back at him. Tomi could read the fear and loathing in her eyes before a single silvery tear escaped and ran down her grubby cheek. Silently, she plopped the container on the floor and tiptoed back.

"He was a pilot. In the war. You are… He says you're a senator. Important. That by holding you, they can fix what's wrong."

Her words troubled him. "But I can't change what has been agreed on. What does he think…" But she'd already turned away and grasped the knob in her hand.

So they think that by abducting me they can…what? Gain some kind of privileges? Change the outcome of the war? The planets that had chosen to join the Federation had done so willingly. His head ached and he rested it against the wooden pole.

"Gods, Gillian, I wish…" He swallowed the words. He'd chosen never to act on his interest before. Now it was all too late. She probably didn't even know he was missing.

Closing his eyes, he conjured up the sight of her—her rich red hair, the vibrant green eyes, her quirky smile. If only he—

A rumble grew beneath his feet and his eyes snapped open. "What's going on?"

The roar grew louder and the floor began to buck. Thuds and shouts alerted him that there was something wrong. A crunching sound filled the air and the boat shimmied hard to the left before returning to its previous situation. Gushing sounds filled the air, replacing the rumble. A shudder rippled through the boards beneath him.

"Barsha!" The swear word erupted from his mouth and he struggled to rise.

The sounds of a ship in distress echoed. It occurred to him that distress was probably a mild word to use, given the list of the boat.

Once again, Tomi tried tugging at his bonds, but they held tight, and the knot in his belly became a coil of snakes. If he didn't get loose quickly, he might be going down with what he suspected was a doomed ship.

The door flung open as a whine of engines split the air before petering away. Clearly, someone had gotten away from the vessel. "Master's gone. I'll release you." The girl, who'd been so terrorized before, now carried a large knife.

For a second, disquiet filled him, but he nodded. He had to get out of there and he was fairly sure she would release him. At least, he hoped that was the plan.

She scurried behind his back like a frightened rabbit. Quick and efficient moves freed his hands and the flow of blood left him hissing as the tearing pain in his shoulders swelled before the worst gradually seeped away.

Tomi moved further from the pole where he'd been secured for hours, grabbing the girl's hand and dragging her. "We need to get out of here."

She let him lead her from the room before stopping and holding her ground. "I can't swim."

Her sudden words had him whipping around. "What?"

She raised her head, fear evident in her eyes. "I can't swim. You must save me."

***

Gillian crowded into the cabin of the scout Carmichael had commandeered on short notice. The tablet remained on her lap and she kept tweaking the code, trying to stay one step ahead of its evolution.

"Whose idea was it to have a morphing code base?" Carmichael groused, and this time, Gillian had to agree. It would have been much simpler if the script hadn't been constantly changing.

"It's so that anyone who does manage to crack it can't follow the wearer of the chrono." *Right now, that is of no help to anyone.* Her stomach was curled into a million hard knots in the pit of her belly. She rubbed her hands surreptitiously over her tummy, but it didn't ease the pain.

"Sir, we are approaching the location given. But, uh, there's a problem." The pilot's voice was perturbed and a million flies took wing in Gillian's stomach.

Carmichael leaned forward and cursed.

"What's wrong?" The mass in Gillian's belly grew worse with the harried words of the pilot. She hunched in his direction, but the bulk of Carmichael's back obscured her view.

"There's a vessel in distress. It's sinking. If that's it…"

Fear clutched her and shook the small amount of comfort she'd derived from helping Carmichael look for Tomi. "The chrono is waterproofed too." She gulped, knowing that he was out there, somewhere in the vast inky blackness of the water. And that it would keep emitting as long as she kept altering the search.

At this time of the year , the sun wouldn't rise until at least ten-thirty or eleven and she shuddered, letting her mind play with the fact that it might already be too late. He could already be dead and floating in the water.

"We'll find him, Carmichael. I know we will. He's resourceful and used to pleasure craft." Kumi's voice shook, but the words offered a modicum of relief to Gillian. Surely, somehow, Kumi would know. *But why should she*, reality whispered. Gillian curled her fingers and the bite of her nails on the fleshy palm of her hand was a lifeline.

The shuttle swooped, its trajectory taking them closer to the water's surface. She could see the ripples and swirls now from the engine of the damaged ship through the large forward window. A dim glow of moonlight flickered and danced on the waves. She sat in her seat, silently willing the craft to move faster. To hurry.

"What is that?" The pilot shifted in his seat and he fiddled with some toggles, the viewing window replaced with a screen. "Increase view five hundred degrees." A grainy image rose, and Gillian's stomach clenched, the bow of a ship sitting proud in the water. "Sir?"

"Is that the ship we are looking for?" Carmichael's voice sounded strained in the now silent cockpit.

"It's in the correct location. But sir, if that's it... It could be too late." The pilot didn't turn around, but he must have realized the atmosphere in the tiny craft was fraught.

"Just do it." Gillian gazed at Carmichael, noting the tension in his shoulders. "Yes, sir."

The scout powered on and Gillian kept her gaze on the screen. Behind her, she could hear the sound of a hiccup as Kumi took in what wasn't said. Carmichael moved, brushing past Gillian. For a moment, she would have given anything for anyone to offer her comfort. But they didn't. She really had no claim on Tomi, except as his past employee, so she concealed her pain and distress, bowed her head over the tablet, and kept working, even though tears blurred her vision.

It seemed like hours until the pilot called out, "Sir, there's someone out there!" She snapped her head up, and behind her, Kumi gasped.

"I'll get the safety harness," Carmichael called.

"Negative, sir. I have men trained for this." The pilot's voice was calm but firm, and Gillian allowed herself a small grin, though that quickly died away. After all, it might not be Tomi.

Even as Gillian scanned the view, she noted that the pilot slipped a headpiece over his ear so he could communicate with the rescue worker. She wished she knew who was in the water, but his words were too low to overhear.

In the main cabin, she could hear bangs and groaning equipment. The scene on the view screen changed to the belly of their craft. She could see a man dangling in the air, and in the water, someone clutching another person. She said a silent prayer that one of them was Tomi. Tension rose in the cabin, thick and heady. The rescuer plunged into the cold waters. A harness was handed over and gripped while the officer dealt with the other. From the movements, Gillian could tell that the person was panicked. Slowly, the first harness rose and she could tell it wasn't Tomi, as the person had long hair and bare legs. She sucked in a breath as the second person in the water was assisted into another harness, then he or she rose with the rescuer. Even though she craned, the outline of the officer obscured her view. She sucked in an unsteady breath, clenched her hands together, and waited.

When Gillian was sure she could last no longer, the door opened with a bang. She quickly looked up, anticipation sizzling along every nerve ending.

There in the doorway was Tomi, wet and shivering, but very much alive. In his arms was a woman, bedraggled and dirty, but he held her so tenderly that any hopes or dreams Gillian harbored melted away. There was never any hope for her and the feelings that burned in her chest.

Without a word, Gillian turned away and fought the sting of tears in her eyes. She noted the sounds of joyous reunion between brother and sister, but she kept her gaze averted, to give them privacy, she piously told herself. When the pilot ordered them strapped in, she breathed a silent sigh of relief. She knew that this torture, him being so close but now forever so far away, would come to an end sooner rather than later.

Just as she was sure she'd be spared, Tomi spoke. "Gillian, thank you for coming to find me."

The clog of tears filled her throat, but she managed to croak, "It was nothing."

"It means a lot to me." He reached out and touched her hand, and she bit back the gasp that rose.

Nerves in her hand jumped and thrummed, but she

ignored them. "Honestly, I'm just pleased I could help." She glanced in his direction, taken aback by the directness in his gaze before the woman beside him shuddered. He scooped her closer and Gillian turned away.

Tomi gripped the edge of the vanity unit and stared at the expression in the mirror, his arms locked. He wanted to go out there and grab Gillian, to shake some emotion into her. She'd all but ignored him on the trip to base, and now, back at Kumi's, she'd physically retreated to another room. His clothes had dried and they were waiting for a couple of Carmichael's men to retrieve a change when he'd excused himself from the slave girl's clinging arms. By the time he'd freed himself, Gillian had disappeared. It felt as if an icy wall existed between them. He'd never experienced that with her before and it was far more than an irritation.

Tap. Tap. The sound of knocking at the door drew his attention. "Who is it?"

"Senator, I have replacement clothes for you. Also, Madam Kumi requests that when you finish, you meet her in her office." The young man on the other side coughed and Tomi raised an eyebrow as he opened the door. Clean clothes were extended and Tomi accepted them with a bow. The earnest face of the officer gave him pause .

"Was there something else, Lieutenant?"

The young officer blushed a deep red. "Madam Kumi was quite adamant. She wishes to see you alone."

Now why would Kumi be adamant about something like that?

"Fine. If you'll let her know I'll be through soon. You may wish to keep—"

"Madam Kumi has already given instructions for the care of the young lady." Once more, Tomi bowed and shut the door. He shucked his ruined gym clothes and pulled on one of his familiar suits. Being dressed in fresh clothing helped to restore some of his balance, but it wouldn't take much to rattle him again .

Even as he opened the door, a wail came from above as the young officer frowned at him. "Sir, she's not very happy about the request to bathe. Miss Edgemont was requested to assist."

Tomi frowned, not sure he was entirely happy with Gillian being put upon like that, but it was Kumi's home and her call. So he left the tiny bathroom and headed in the direction of her study. The door was open and she sat at the desk, her face wreathed with smiles.

"Oh, Tomi, I'm so glad you're home and safe." She rose and crossed the room, her arms outstretched.

Tomi tugged the door shut behind them and let her hug him tight. "Well, I have to be honest, I'm inordinately glad to be here too. But what was so important that you needed to send me a message?"

Her face settled into a frown. "You aren't going to be too happy. It's about Gillian." She indicated he take a seat. He almost wished he could refuse, but the entreaty in her face told him she was worried, so he sat on the chair nearest. "Oh dear, I'm not even totally sure where to start."

"At the beginning seems wisest."

For a moment Kumi smiled, but it melted away. "You know the situation with her brother? Well, it seems the effects are far more wide reaching than any of us expected. She's got problems of a kind that are only going to get bigger. Carmichael heard that her home was searched last night."

Tomi half rose out of his seat. "What?"

"Carmichael is doing everything he can to shield her, but… I know she didn't have anything to do with her brother's plan to assassinate me, but as a sister to a convicted conspirator… She's in an unenviable position right now, Tomi. Things are only going to get worse until we find the perpetrator. And she's alone. No one is standing in her corner. I mean, she has a family but… I can't do that publicly, you know that, but you can. You have to."

Hearing Kumi say the words was like a physical blow. Kumi was right. He knew Gillian was innocent—he'd bet his life on that truth. But it left her open to suspicion. It was why she'd been dismissed. *But that she is alone?* He'd seen images of her and her frail mother attending the hearing. He knew her father suffered from ill health, which kept him away. His heart ached for Gillian as confusion and frustration warred within him.

"So what do you propose?" He leaned forward, resting his elbows on his knees.

Kumi smiled and just as he was sure she was about to speak, the door burst open and the girl—hell, he still didn't even know her name—came stalking in. "You let her…" She thrust out a hand, indicating an angry, wet, and bloody Gillian who stood in the doorway. "You let her wet me!" There was outrage and fear in the voice. Much as he wanted to go to Gillian, right now the shivering waif before him needed to be settled.

He held out a hand and she dropped to the floor, crawling over, and the humiliating way she effaced herself turned his heart. She settled herself against his leg and looked up. When he glanced up to his sister, Kumi wasn't watching him or the girl. Her face was grave and staring at the doorway. When he glanced that way, it was empty. "Who? Gillian?"

"She's gone, Tomi."

He closed his eyes and exhaled heavily. "I'm never going to get this right." Even as he muttered the words, he accepted the truth, and his heart weighed heavily in his chest.

"Oh, I wouldn't give up quite so soon, brother. She loves you. I'm sure of that."

He attempted to sit up straight in his chair. "What do you mean?"

"She was pretty quick to get here after I told her what had happened to you. And I know she was beside herself with worry, not that she wanted anyone to know. But you have to tell her, show her. Otherwise you'll never know, will you?"

"But it was you her brother was convicted of attempting to assassinate. It's not something…" Even as he watched, Kumi rolled her eyes at him.

"Oh, don't be so stuffy, Tomi! Even with that, she cares about you. I'll tell you something though, you're going to have to be quick if you want a future with her. She's been pretty much written off here on Reunion. She'll have to leave to get any kind of a future, and you know it. The longer you take getting around to whatever you plan to do, the more chances you're going to be too damned late." Kumi stood up with a jerk and turned in the direction of the big window. "I love you, Tomi, but right now you're so damned…male!" With the parting shot, she strode from the room.

Gillian clambered into her vehicle, refusing to look back. "That's my past." But it didn't help that her voice wobbled or her stomach roiled. The fact that it felt like her heart was being ripped out added to her overall misery.

The car climbed into the sky and she guided it toward home, in need of something to focus on. When her house loomed, she landed softly and hurried from within to her front door. "Hey, Ma? I'm back!" The empty residence echoed and she moved from room to room. Finally, in the bedroom her mother had been using, she found a note.

Gone home to Father. Call me when you're ready.

Alone. Again. If anyone had asked her, she knew she wouldn't be able to explain why this hit her so hard. After all, even with the mess her brother had left for her to deal with, she'd never felt so low.

Her hands gripped the paper, her fingers scrunching it tightly as she sank to the floor, dry-eyed. A cold knot formed in her chest, squeezing the air from her lungs. She refused to cry though. That would be weak, and never in her life had anyone called her that.

Time passed and she breathed through the anguish. Gillian let it swell for a while then shoved it firmly away. Giving in wouldn't help now. "Time to find where I belong now." She uncurled her fingers, wincing at the slight tug of pain.

Pushing up from the floor was an effort as her bones felt stiff and frozen. A glance out the window told her hours had elapsed while she'd huddled in a heap by the bed. Deep in her mind came the reminder that she should eat, but even that held no interest.

"You can't sit on your backside feeling sorry for yourself. That has never fixed anything. Time to act, Gillian. You can do it." She did, moving to the small tablet device, quickly clicking through to the positions vacant. She would no longer be eligible for Star Corps or Naval Fleet, a fact which limited her employment prospects. "What else can I do?" She only knew her role and computer sciences. Surely there was someone who needed her skill set?

Gillian bit her lip as she scanned the options. The pickings were certainly slim, but one caught her eye. *Assistant to Chief Communication Officer, Vega II.*

It wasn't startling and it was at the end of the Federation's reach, but it was more than she currently had. Even more importantly, it put her a vast distance from Tomi. Reading through their requirements didn't take long at all, and she was pleasantly surprised with the remuneration package too.

Gillian snapped up a tiny mirror from the drawer, gave a quick brush of her fingers through her hair, and tidied away the worst of the mess. Then she gave a silent sigh of relief. "At least my eyes aren't red from crying!" One breath then another supplied the oxygen to calm her. Her face felt flushed, but she hoped they would think it was purely nerves from applying. Then she gave a decisive nod. "I'm ready to do this." She slid the mirror back into its place.

Her hand wobbled as she quickly keyed in the advertised connection and waited. The planetary distances had, thankfully, been breached over a century ago, and not for the first time she wondered how the settlers of Reunion had coped with the long periods of no contact.

The screen lit up and a face appeared. A woman,

maybe in her fifth decade, smiled into the communicator camera. "Chief Communications Office, Vega II."

"Hi, my name is Gillian Edgemont and I'd like to apply for the assistant's position. I have experience in both office procedures and computational sciences. I'm happy to give you my identification number so you can verify." The words gushed out like a river and the woman at the other end laughed.

"Hang on, kiddo. The position is open immediately, but we are a long way from anywhere. You do realize that, don't you?" The woman seemed to be scrutinizing her, but Gillian nodded.

"I do, and I'm available now. Let me key in my details and you can read my background. There is one small thing though—" Gillian tapped in the details as the woman cut her off.

"Honey, if you can do half the things this report says, the details of your dismissal won't be worth concerning ourselves with. But look, let me check this over and get back to you in an hour or two."

The screen blurred and turned black, and Gillian dropped into the seat beside the desk. "What have I done?" She dragged an unsteady hand through her hair as her stomach jumbled wildly. But she couldn't—wouldn't— change her mind. She'd made a commitment to create a new life, and if that meant on Vega II, then so be it .

On that thought, she stood and turned away from the device. She planned to pack, whichever way this went.

Chapter 3

"What do you mean, she's left? Where the hell has she gone?" Tomi stalked over to the window and looked out. Kumi's words echoed in his mind.

The longer you take getting around to whatever you plan to do, the more chances you're going to be too damned late. Of course, Kumi had been right. Hearing that Gillian had left Reunion shocked him. He'd honestly thought there had been time. How wrong he'd been.

He gazed sightless out over the city before him. It had all been there a mere fingertip away, but he'd vacillated and she'd left. The only woman he'd ever love. It wasn't right. In fact...

He whirled around, facing the woman who waited anxiously. "Tell me what you know, Iyana."

"Sir, she left on a shuttle. I believe she is bound for Vega II. Apparently, there was a position..." His new assistant, Iyana, was capable enough, but she didn't anticipate his needs the way Gillian had. She didn't smile at him each morning when she brought him his coffee and files. There wasn't a spark that lit in his chest every time she was near. Unfair of him, though it was, to measure Iyana against Gillian, he couldn't help the comparison. And Iyana failed.

"Find out exactly where and when. Then get me on the next damned shuttle." He clenched his fists, controlling the burning anger that ate at him.

Iyana's eyes opened wide, the whites startlingly stark against her dark, chocolate skin tone. Her fingers coiled in the long ropes of Illurian pearls that twisted around her throat.

"Sir? I don't…" Iyana sounded confused, but for the first time, he didn't give a damn about being a senator or the important work he was doing. He needed to find Gillian—tell her how he loved her. To bring her home.

"Do it, Iyana. Then clear my calendar."

"But, sir! The senate is due to meet—"

Tomi bristled. "Right now, I don't care. Get me a seat on that damned shuttle. Then get the team together to sort out a workable solution." He was being unreasonable, but urgency clawed at him. Gillian was alone. If anyone knew who she was, who her brother was…

"Uh, your sister called too. The girl is asking after you, and Madam Kumi says she has news." Iyana stood in the doorway, a frown on her face as she clutched a sheaf of papers to her chest.

Those words stopped him in his tracks. Yet another responsibility. The girl had become like a creeping vine, twining herself around him. But right now, he just wanted clear air to go to Gillian. Fate was obviously conspiring against him though.

"Fine, I'll call her now." Frustration built like a bubble, and the sensation of drowning echoed through his consciousness. Tapping the console, he frowned. *What the hell am I supposed to do with the girl now?*

"Kumi? You were looking for me?"

"I was… Well, actually, Carmichael was. We have news, good and bad."

He waited and Carmichael's visage filled the screen. "Fine, get on with it then."

Carmichael quirked an eyebrow at him and Tomi dragged his fingers through his hair. "Sorry. It's just…"

"She's left. Yes, we are aware of that. I've had a man tailing her for some time. After her assistance with finding the perpetrator of the attacks on Kumi, I have expected someone would try for her."

Tomi's stomach bottomed out. "What do you mean?" He leaned closer to the console. "Why would someone?"

"Because of her brother? Maybe they think there is a perceived connection to you? Honestly, Tomi, at this point we don't know why. It's just…" Carmichael stopped, sighed heavily, and rubbed a hand across his stubbled chin. "With the way her home has been targeted for searches, someone is tipping off the local authorities."

Tomi went still. *Her home had been targeted for searches?* No one had mentioned this before. He knew her home had been searched once. "Why the hell didn't you tell me, Carmichael? Kumi knows…" His heart pounded in his chest.

"How you feel? Yes, she does, but my hands are tied, Tomi. Of all people, you should appreciate that there are times when I'm bound by my oath to the naval authorities. Now, with that in mind, I've ensured she is protected as much as I can. But I *feel*—and it's purely a gut reaction— that something is about to give. In the case of your kidnapping, we are also sure it's tied to the ongoing incursions against the Federation. Reunion is the jewel in the crown of the Federation, so it makes sense for them to continue to focus on this planet. But whoever took you clearly has a vested interest in damaging Reunion from the top down".

Tomi calmed himself and focused on his breathing. He was going to Vega II to bring Gillian home. "I'm going after her, Carmichael. I have my staff making the necessary plans."

A knock sounded on Tomi's office door and he glanced quickly toward it. There was Iyana waiting for him. He nodded once, acknowledging her presence, before turning back to the screen.

"Damn it all, Tomi. You stay right where you are, " Carmichael demanded. Tomi just smiled. "I'll talk to you later." Then he turned the communicator off.

Arrival on Vega II was surreal, Gillian decided. She had learned that the tiny planet was obscured by several moons, meaning that the days were short and interspersed only with brief patches of daylight hours. "What have I done?"

Her bags were shoved onto an air trolley as she clambered down the cold steps of the shuttle. The cramped conditions she'd endured aboard the shuttle for the last three weeks were only marginally improved here, she noted with a grimace. The spacious atmosphere dome featured bright red struts and intermittent alcoves painted neon yellow. They were signed as emergency life capsules. She didn't know what she'd expected, but it certainly wasn't this. The journey had been spent in introspection and tutelage in the ways of atmosphere dome security and living.

Nothing prepared her for the barrenness that stretched out before her, the utilitarian surroundings and the lack of green grass. Even the air was devoid of anything homely, tasting stale on her tongue.

"Miss Edgemont? Gillian?" The woman who she'd been dealing with since applying for the job was waving her arms from within the security lounge , her face wreathed in smiles. "It's so good to have you here finally. Now let's collect your things and I can take you to your accommodations."

The fast talking woman left Gillian reeling. "Yeah, I only have a few bags."

"That's fine, Gillian. I may call you that, can't I? Of course, I'm Elvira, and you'll be sharing my office. It's so good to have another woman on the team. This place is a little 'male oriented' if you get my meaning."

Elvira grasped the handles of the suitcases and hauled them up as if they were light. Gillian felt sick, realizing that she'd accepted this posting for the next six, very long months. It was going to be an excruciating time, and she hoped that unwelcome and unaccustomed claustrophobia didn't get her between now and then.

"Your room is in the nearest wing. We need to be able to get to the communications center quickly. But don't worry about that today, there's plenty of time to think about work tomorrow."

Gillian let Elvira talk while they walked. The distance wasn't that far, yet it felt like being escorted to her execution. The hallway was, she'd read, a life support tube, which had sufficient oxygen and supplies to keep fifty alive for six weeks, but it felt like it was shrinking around her, cutting off her air.

"You are okay, aren't you, Gillian? Living in an

enclosed atmosphere isn't for everyone." Elvira pushed the door open and stared at her.

"I'll be fine. I just need a decent sleep and to start work." The smile she gave was false; she could feel it stretching across her face, and Elvira was obviously not convinced.

"Well… If you say so. I'll pop by for you in the morning and help you find the office and your way around. If you need anything, I'm extension five-one-zero-nine, dear. Now a quick shower, unpack, and bed is probably your best plan."

Gillian shut the door behind the woman and heaved her bags to the bed. She unpacked as quickly as she could, refusing to think as she shoved clothes into the small chest of drawers then dumped the empty cases on the floor. With a sigh, Gillian slumped onto the bed of her appointed accommodations.

The communicator on the bedside buzzed and she picked up the handset without thinking. "Hello?"

"Gillian, it's Kumi here. Kumi Ito. Look, it's not really… I shouldn't have called, but you needed to be warned. Tomi is on his way."

Stunned, Gillian gaped as the base unit, her mouth open. The butterflies she thought she'd conquered took flight in her belly.

"Gillian, are you there?"

"I… Yes. But why? Why is he coming here? I mean…" The words were barely coherent and her mind whirled. *He's coming here? To Vega II?*

"Because he's a fool in love, Gillian." Kumi's voice softened. "After you left… Once he knew, he had his team cancel everything, every appointment. He organized to catch the next shuttle, but he couldn't find one. He was beside himself. So he chartered one. He could be there as early as tomorrow." Then there was silence.

Gillian covered her mouth with her wobbling hand.

"You do love him, don't you?"

Tears pricked Gillian's eyes. "I… Yes, Kumi, I do. I always have, but he's never shown—"

"He's a man, Gillian. One who was taught about responsibility from a very young age. Our father and grandfather constantly told him that he had a great and important future on Reunion as they did with Ren. So he's always put that before his own needs and those closest. It's not a fault, it's just him. If you love him, give him a chance. Please."

Scalding tears escaped, dribbling their way down her cheeks. "He never said. Not once."

"Men don't, and you should know that by now."

Gillian found herself smiling at Kumi's truculent words. "So how did you find out then?" She gave a sniffle and rolled her eyes at the way she was behaving. *You'd think this is my first crush.*

"With Tomi, it was easy. He's been like a cat on a hot tin roof around you since you first appeared. With Carmichael? It wasn't that simple. Much like you, I didn't trust myself or my emotions. Gillian, if you want Tomi, you're going to have to take a chance."

Kumi was right. "Yeah, I know. Look, I need to go now. I have lots to do." *And lots to think about.*

"Not a problem. Just don't tell Tomi I called. He thinks I get too involved in his affairs as it is." With that, Kumi broke the connection and Gillian couldn't help a smile at her parting words, but it faded away. *If only it was all that simple.*

Tomi's heart rate spiked. Walking through the cavernous tubes to the communications center via the residential section was intriguing, and he arched his neck here and there.

He'd been on space stations and other planets in the course of his work, but none had been so utilitarian in nature. Vega II had only recently been colonized, now that the Federation scientists had the atmosphere dome technology locked down. Previously, it had been very hit or miss, with some tragedies during the early testing phases. But knowing how far the science had come didn't make him feel any more secure.

"Sir, watch the cording." The guard who'd been assigned to Tomi touched his shoulder. Tomi blinked. The area they were walking through was under secondary construction since Vega II was also the home of the Federation's terra forming experiments. "I'm sorry, I was thinking."

"Yes, sir. It's just, while they're working, it's important to be aware." The young officer's cautionary words brought Tomi up. He was right of course .

"Where is the communication section housed?"

"Oh, it's just ahead, sir. I'll take you there once we have you settled in a set of rooms." Tomi really didn't give a frig whether he had a suite or not. He just wanted to see Gillian, assure himself of her safety. Then, maybe, he could convince her to come home. Except this time, home meant to him. Suddenly his lips and mouth dried .

So close and yet still so far to go, his mind whispered. *I will make her believe me.* But what if she didn't share his feelings? His stomach bottomed out.

Kumi was rarely wrong about such things. The fluttering of a million tiny butterfly wings took flight in his belly. *What if I'm wrong?*

The officer stopped. "This will be your accommodation, sir. Next door is Elvira Durane , and on the other, the new communications officer. I have to say, she's a looker."

The words intruded on Tomi's consciousness. "A looker?"

"Yeah, she's gorgeous with deep red hair. Most of the guys think she's the hottest thing we've ever had on Vega II."

"Really? And her name would be?"

"Gillian Edgemont. The rest of the officers are taking bets at who will hook up with her." Tomi didn't like the turn this conversation was taking.

"Well, I'm sure she's here to do a job, not participate in the sexploits of Vega II."

The young officer looked stunned and a bright red crest colored his cheeks. Tomi almost felt sorry. His tone had been cutting, but to think of them seeing Gillian like that...There was very little respect, and he'd be pleased to get her away from here. Back to Reunion, but this time in the safety of his arms.

"Sir. Yes, sir." Coming to attention, the young man opened the door. "The office isn't far from here."

This time, they moved at a brisk pace without any verbal commentary , and within minutes they stood at the large entryway. Tomi was ushered into the security zone and waved through on presentation of his credentials.

"Sir, if you'll come this way." A large, chocolate skinned woman smiled at him. "My name is Elvira, and I believe you are here to see——"

"Gillian Edgemont. Yes. We will need some privacy.

There is a free office?" The woman frowned deeply. "Well…"

"It's important I speak to her on a matter of urgency."

"Of course, Senator. I'll take you through to the private meeting room." She opened a door and led him down a long hallway, his footsteps clattering on the metal flooring. The woman opened a door at the end and he took in the utilitarian room filled with a long metal meeting table and modular seating. "I'll get Gillian for you."

He knew she wasn't happy about the situation, but he didn't care. Gillian was close by and waiting was difficult. He lowered himself into a seat, only to find his foot jiggling. He stood, pacing in one direction then the other. A notice on the wall caught his eye and he'd just stepped up to it when the door opened.

"Senator Ito? You wanted to see me?"

He turned suddenly and there she was, framed in the doorway. Her cheeks pink, her eyes sparkling. Everything he could ever ask for.

***

The handle of the door was cold as Gillian prepared herself. Thankfully, Elvira hadn't felt the need to accompany her, so she had time. One deep breath then another. Gods, she hoped Kumi was right.

With great care, she twisted the knob and pushed the door open. He was looking at the wall. "Senator Ito? You wanted to see me?" She nearly cursed her own clumsiness at the poor greeting.

"Gillian." He sounded strangled and, for the first time since she'd met him, there was an uncertainty about him.

One step into the room, then another while she gazed at him.

"The door?" His voice broke the trance she'd lost herself in and she nodded before reaching out and shutting it with a bang.

"Come here, please."

Gillian complied in silence. When she was finally face to face with him, she gazed deeply into his eyes. "What are we——"

"I missed you. You left without even saying goodbye."

Her stomach quivered as the breath of his words whispered over her lips. "I…"

"Why did you leave? Why did you leave me behind?"

"I didn't think it was important to you. I mean… I work… I *worked* for you, but that was all." How much should she tell him? Spilling her guts about the depths of her feelings without something to guide her seemed both silly and overly ambitious.

He watched her, his brown eyes flicking from side to side as if he were trying to read her face. "Was it, Gillian?" The words were soft and drugging, rather like the taste of his breath. His lips were so close, and she could see the tiny flecks in his eyes.

"I… What do you want from me?" She couldn't stop the whispered question and he smiled.

"Are you ready for the answer? Because once I give that, I can't go back and neither can you." His hand shook as it touched her cheek lightly.

"Yes. Give me the answer."

He smiled, full lips tugging up at the corners, and she was sure they found some corresponding bit of her heart and the tiny muscles in the depths of her being. "I want everything. I want…" He inhaled deeply, his eyes closing involuntarily, as if he were welcoming her very essence.

Her knees turned watery and she put out a hand, seeking support. It found his arm and clutched.

"Gillian." His eyes opened and gazed at her. She drowned, lost in their connection, as he slowly caressed her cheek.

He's going to kiss me! It was a shriek of exultation that reverberated through her mind. Her breathing shallower, she swayed in his direction.

Knock. Knock.

Gillian sprang away and watched his face even as she answered the summons. "Who… Who is it?"

"It's Elvira, dear. May I come in?"

Tomi—'Senator Ito' her beleaguered mind shouted— didn't look impressed. His mouth flattened and his eyes sparked with anger. "Uh, yes. Come in."

The door slid open with a squeak and Gillian glanced at the woman as Tomi spoke. "Ma'am?"

"Senator, given the time, the chief communications officer asked me to relay an invitation to join him for lunch."

The woman had worked out there was a strong emotion in the air. Gillian nearly giggled at the situation. Even a blind man could see there was something going on!

"If you could please inform the CCO that I must decline. I need to talk at length with Miss Edgemont. However, if we could arrange for catering at my suite…"

"It's automated in the room. Gillian knows how to work it." Elvira smiled knowingly.

Gillian started at his words. "But… Sir, I have work."

"Nonsense. You go along with the nice senator and we'll catch up later."

Elvira bustled from the room, but not before Gillian caught the double entendre. *Catch up? She wants to wring every bit of gossip from me.*

As the door shut, Tomi strode forward. "Lock it."

Her breath caught. "What?"

"I said, lock the door."

Used to following his instructions, she did. Before she could turn, his hands clasped her shoulders and spun her back to face him. "Now, to continue…" His lips descended and touched hers.

Gillian's soft lips were finally beneath his. They were full and luscious. They were mobile as he moved tentatively, learning their contours.

The touch of her fingers wrapping themselves into the lapel of his jacket made him feel like a king. Gillian was in his arms and it was right.

For several long moments, he wallowed in the sensations of holding her close, of tasting her, and after she opened her mouth, the deep moist cavern of honey. Then reality intruded and he pulled away. She shivered and he smiled at the hectic color that flushed her cheeks.

"What?" She stepped back slowly, raising her fingertips to her lips. "Why did… Oh my Gods! Kumi said something, didn't she?"

He frowned. Why would Gillian's first thoughts be for Kumi? A suspicion formed. "Why did you just ask about Kumi? Have you been in contact with her?"

Gillian answered him with a guilty look and duck of her head.

Frustration rose, burning him. "Damn it all. Why did you talk to Kumi and not me?"

"I… How was I…" She turned away and shook her head. "I don't even know what this means. You turn up here and kiss me. Is this supposed to be a visit with benefits? Official? Unofficial?"

Her words pained him on every level. Everything she asked was valid. But it hurt that she had to ask. "Gillian, stand still and—"

She whirled around. Her eyes flashed a deep emerald and he was entranced. *What?*

"To be honest, when Kumi contacted me—"

"She contacted you? When?"

Gillian stilled, her chest moving rapidly as she sucked in oxygen. Her face shone pink with embarrassment. "Look, she contacted me. It was pretty much right after I got here. She wanted to let me know you were on the way."

"So you knew." *Blast Kumi and her interfering ways!* Anger coursed hot and heady, and he was determined, some day soon, he'd call his sister to account. *It isn't any of her bloody business!*

"So who else knew I was coming? Did you setup the young officer? That bloody Elvira?"

"What do you mean about… No!" Gillian backed away. "I don't know what you want. Kumi just wanted to let me know that you would be here."

He felt hurt that Kumi thought she should meddle. He growled and blinked, attempting to wash off his anger.

"What's the time?" He glanced at his chrono, but was struck that he really didn't have a clue as to the time here on Vega II.

"It's thirteen hundred. I can show you to the officer's mess if you'd like."

She spoke stiffly, and he sighed, aware he'd insulted her. He needed to weigh his options, and had a fair suspicion that by now, tongues would be wagging. "No, I think it's best you and I talk in privacy."

Gillian frowned and opened her mouth before he raised a hand. "Trust me, there are things we need to discuss."

Gillian nodded. "So where are you staying?"

"Next door to you." A spurt of pleasure jolted him as she glanced up, obviously startled.

She huffed. "Okay then. Let's get out of here."

Gillian wrenched on the door and he smiled, once more entranced in the sight of her delectable form leading the way. As always in the past, his gaze dipped to her derriere and he imagined it naked with his fingers gripping the soft skin. He started to sweat and his body reacted, tightened, and began the deep throb that he associated with her .

Making their way across the quadrangle took very little time, and soon they were at his room. He fished in his pocket for the small key device he'd been given and it slid open. "Come on in and we can order something to eat."

The door closed behind them and he looked around. "How do I…"

Gillian smiled, though it was only a ghost. "Let me do it." She made her way to a tiny communicator in the corner of the main room. "It's Gillian Edgemont in Senator Ito's suite. I'd like to place an order."

Tomi tuned out, watching the way she grinned and toyed with a loose strand of red hair. Her style was different, he noted with surprise.

She wore a communications uniform of black, but it molded to her body like a glove, outlining her delicious curves. She'd lost weight recently. She hadn't had what he'd consider extra padding, but now she'd become finer, more delicate and, to his mind, fragile. Her hair wasn't in its usual knot either; instead, it was loosely tied back with a clip. It made her seem more approachable and sexier than ever. None of these thoughts were helping as his body ached.

"Are you okay, Senator?"

He realized she'd been watching him for some time. "Yes, but you've changed."

Gillian colored and he was delighted. "Well, different environment. Here I'm not running a senator's office. I'm just…"

His happy mood was chased away. "I didn't want you to go. I fought it, you know."

Gillian turned her back on him. "I didn't. It hurt that you didn't talk to me. It was a slap in the face." When she looked in his direction once more, the pain in her eyes speared him.

He stepped forward, hoping he'd read the emotion in her eyes correctly. "You'll never know just how much it hurt me to let you go like that. Then the abduction…"

"Oh my gods! I forgot!" She stepped away, paler than before. "Your girl, is she well?" Her voice frosted as if she's just raised a glacial wall between them and he tensed. "Of course, I shouldn't be here. I'll leave you now."

Confusion filled him. *What the hell is wrong now?* "Don't you dare leave. Not again." He barked the orders and she stopped in her tracks, but this time she didn't look at him. Her shoulders were set and tight, and he longed to reach out and soothe whatever new complication she'd imagined. "Sit down, we need to talk."

The long sigh she gave was weary and he knew there were demons that he couldn't even see to fight right now. He needed to know, so he could defeat them. Only working through the problem, methodically, could make that happen.

A beeping sound caught his attention. "What's that?"

"The meal is ready." Next to the communications unit was a small door, which she opened. Two meals, complete with drinks, waited. She picked up one tray and carried it to the table. He collected the other tray as the door shut.

"So. What do you wish to discuss?" Gillian had just picked up her fork when the address system squawked.

"Incoming vessel of unknown origin. Vega II to level one lockdown!" Klaxons started to wail and Tomi half rose as the lockdown sequence whirred into life.

Chapter 4

"Oh my gods! What's going on?" Fear clogged Gillian's throat as her heart pounded. Tomi stood and moved to the communications center, his movements unhurried and graceful.

Before he could touch the screen, the room rocked and she held her hand out, grasping the table. "Are we… Do you think we're under attack?"

"All personnel. Proceed to the nearest life preservation point immediately." The address system crackled and popped, and Gillian was unable to control the gasp that rose or the frisson of fear.

"Gillian? Where's the preservation point?" He strode in her direction and took her hand. "Gillian! Come on, this is important. Preservation point? Where?"

"Bed… Bedroom. Each bedroom is equipped with…"

He cursed and gripped her hand before he dragged her in the direction of the sleeping quarters.

She looked around as she let him propel her to the larger sleeping area. It had to be at least twice the size of hers.

"Don't lose it just yet, sweetheart. Get on and settle in before the oxygen tube encloses with me on the outside."

"Pod closure in ten seconds." The words intoned and heightened her sense of panic.

Her startled gaze met his. "Oh… Yes." She quickly scrambled onto the soft mattress and felt the dip as he crawled on beside her. Then a hiss broke through the wail of sirens. A section of metal deployed and they were encapsulated in a large tube. She'd read how it worked, but reality was nothing like she imaged. The bed had now become a life vessel.

"Pod enclosure successful. Pod reopening in six hours unless manual override is engaged." Then there was silence. The capsule rocked again then stilled. Whatever was going on outside, they were safe, unless something shattered its reinforced skin.

Gillian stared at the inside, unable to suppress a shiver. "Six hours is a long time." Her stomach wobbled at the thought. Until reaching Vega II, she'd never thought of herself as claustrophobic, but this time it was different. Six hours in an enclosed tube with Tomi…

"Are you cold?" He tugged up the covers over them as she shook her head.

"Not really, just scared. Even with the attacks on Reunion during the war, there was never anything like this. I mean…"

"I know." His hand rubbed lightly up and down her arm, and even in the midst of the scary situation, her body tightened and nipples peaked. She gulped, hoping that the increased oxygen flow would clear her mind, but instead she was swamped in his scent. The close quarters were testing her emotional defenses.

"Really, I thought we were past all this." She waved her hands in the air and he grabbed one, holding it tight.

"There are still Indies out there. They'd destroy our Federation and the peace that we enjoy."

Those like my brother. She closed her eyes at the pain such a thought wrought on her system. *He'll forever thrust us apart and it hurts, damn it!* It wasn't even a choice she'd had any control over.

"Gillian? I know you aren't involved. That you never were. I wanted to protect you."

Her head swung in his direction. "What do you mean?"

"When Kumi said your house had been searched, I was beyond furious. I wish you'd told me."

"The Central Registry told me I wasn't to contact you. They said if they determined I had, I wouldn't find work on Reunion. So I didn't. Besides which, once my employment was terminated…" She shrugged, trying to keep the action nonchalant.

"Oh, Gillian." He leaned in and she told herself it meant nothing, but when his lips touched her skin, she moved, needing the reassurance of his embrace. She opened to him, hungry for the comfort he offered.

His hands slid behind her back, pulling her closer, and she couldn't fight the warm, fluttery feelings that filled her.

"Gillian." He groaned against her mouth and the weakness and sense of melting increased. Her core shot to white-hot and the fire that had burned for so long seeped out of her pores. Between her legs pulsed an emptiness that only he could assuage.

Their movements turned urgent as fingers twined in strands of hair and tugged each other closer so that their bodies nestled in an intimate embrace. His lips skated against hers before trailing over her cheekbone and down her arched neck, finding the sweet spot at her collarbone. Her hands found his shirt, tugging it loose from his pants, then burrowed below to the warm flesh. Hard and hot. The need rose up, overwhelming her. The air became close and the only sounds were their panting breaths.

Her shirt popped free, the zipper sliding away like melting butter so that the cloth parted, leaving her bra as the only covering over the heaving mounds of her breasts. She bowed up, wanting his touch, needing more than he had given so far.

"Gillian, we have to slow down."

Her heart rate spiked. "You don't…" Confusion filled her. He'd nearly had her naked. He'd been feasting on her naked skin, now he wanted to stop? Was she wrong? Gillian scooted as far away as she could in the pod. "Oh gods! I'm… This shouldn't have…" She couldn't stand to look at him as she burned with shame. *What have I nearly done?*

Huddled in the corner, she trembled and scrabbled at the fasteners.

"No. I mean, this time, I want you to be sure, not just some furtive incendiary sex. I want you. All of you, Gillian." He reached out, but she flinched.

Molten hot shame filled her. How could she have forgotten? He was a senator and she a convict's sister. "Oh, right. Forgive me if I find that a little unbelievable, Senator. After all, you stopped us when I was ready to beg you for more. Incendiary? Yes. Not thought out, dreamed of, or desired for a long time? Yeah, I don't think so." Gillian bit back the moan and chewed at her lip. She knew she sounded bitter and winced. *Way to go, Gillian. Just tell him everything!*

"Damn it, if I didn't want you, I wouldn't have

followed you to Vega II. But I'm here and dying to sink myself into your luscious body, sweetheart. You, Gillian, are my total reason for this trip."

"Then why stop? Is it her?" she sobbed, wanting desperately to believe his words. But the specter of the girl, the way he'd cradled her tenderly flashed into her brain. *How could I have forgotten that?*

"Her? Her, who?" He seemed genuinely confused, but it didn't make her feel any better.

"The girl from the boat. You know, the one you saved? I thought…" She wanted to call back her words, but it was too late.

He smiled, and the look was hot. "Jealous, are you? Sweetheart, for all I feel responsible, she doesn't keep me up at night and so damned turned on I have to shower three times a day. It's you I want. Now come here, if you're sure you want me."

Her heart thudded, slowly as if coated by warm honey. Could she trust his words? Taking a deep breath, she moved, scooting closer before sinking into his embrace. She knew exactly what he wanted.

Gillian sank into Tomi's arms and he thanked the gods that she trusted him. Not that he'd hurt a hair on her head, but her pride and self-respect had taken a beating in the last few months. He certainly hadn't helped his cause with the other girl, and he grieved that he'd carelessly made things worse.

In the dim, recessed lighting, he saw the strands of red silky hair fan out and the slight smile on her face. "You know, I've dreamed of you like this. In my arms. A million times I nearly said something." Feelings coursed. This time, he'd tell her everything.

"Tomi, you should have. I mean…" Her whisper sent shivers through him, stirring the fire that burned within his gut.

He frowned. "I wasn't sure. You never gave any indication."

Her laugh was throaty. "Well, neither did you." She lifted her hand and gently caressed his face. Their gazes caught.

A frisson of desire shot through him, centering in his heart. Pressure pooled in his groin, and his erection jerked uncomfortably. He banked the hunger, desperate to do this right, for both of them. "It was remiss of me not to let you know. But I'm a man, and we don't take failure, particularly like this, well."

"Failure?"

"You left, didn't you?" He bent down, placing a soft kiss on the tip of her chin. "I should have told you, every day, how beautiful you are." He touched the tip of her slightly tilted nose. "How much I appreciate every tiny gesture of caring you showed." Tomi's eyes zeroed in on her mouth. "How much I desire you."

Their lips met. Gently at first, but the raging torrent of need flooded his entire body. It became rapacious and his mouth plundered, his tongue questing. Gillian gave back, kiss-for-kiss, and soon they were gasping for breath as hands traversed each other's bodies, needing to learn the dips and nuances.

His fingers found the soft curves of her breast and curled over it. "So beautiful."

She arched in. At his touch, the tips of her nipples distended, and this time he searched for and found the zipper. It gave a gentle ripping sound as it descended. Her bra, the palest of peaches, was dull next to her beautiful, sweat-slicked skin. This time, he was determined to peel it away to uncover the prize that lay beneath.

"Tomi, you, you won't stop this. Oh, don't stop!"

His fingers toyed playfully with the nubbin covered by satin, and she writhed beneath him. He burned to do more, the ache in his groin stealing his breath. "Oh,I don't intend stopping this time."

With careful touches, he found the clasp between the mounds and freed her. Raspberry nipples called to him and he leaned in to taste her. Sweet flesh furled tighter against his tongue and lips. He suckled hard and she cried out, arching once more. Her flesh was soft and smelled faintly of her floral scent, sending his arousal skyrocketing.- More. He needed so much more.

"*Utsukushii.*" The language of his forebears rose instinctively. In his mind, he told her how beautiful she was as he pushed the layers of fabric away, and she writhed against him, legs splayed. Without conscious thought, he crawled between them, yanking on his clothing, hungry for the touch of skin to skin.

He thrust his hand up and it hit the metallic lid of their shared pod. "Shit!" The momentary shock of pain pushed the fog of desire from his brain.

She giggled softly. "Are you okay?"

He grimaced with embarrassment as his gaze traveled over her. He let his mind feast on the beauty of her for an instant then hovered closer, once more needing her kiss as if it were the nectar of life.

Gillian groaned into his mouth, the sound both hungry and excited, as she twined her arms around him, tugging him closer. This time, when he pulled back, his gaze found and gloried in the flush of red on her skin, the feverish glitter of her eyes, and the swollen lips.

"I need you naked."

She pushed her hands down, seeking the fasteners on her pants, but he brushed them away. She frowned, and he growled. "This is my job."

The smile she gifted him with stole his breath. "Well, since I can't do that, I'm sure I can find another way to help." Then her clever hands found the button and zipper of his pants and his mind blanked.

———

The feel of Tomi's hands and mouth on her body was drugging. The soft touches dragged at her mind. Her nerves skittered at each glancing caress. Heat rolled through her belly and her blood surged in her veins. She was vibrantly aware of his every movement, yet her eyes stayed at a somnolent half-mast, heavy with the pleasure he was sharing.

Even the act of pushing her clothes away, stripping her bare, caught her breath and left her gasping and sucking down the scent-laden oxygen.

"Oh gods, more!" she chanted as her panties and trousers caught at her ankles. The whisper of his breath fluttered against her intimate flesh and she couldn't contain the moan that erupted.

His laugh, dark and liquid, became a possessive growl. "You are exquisite, Gillian. Truly a gift from the gods." His lips touched her hip and she jerked, senses wound tight. The molten fire buried deep within her body burned her loins. She rocked against him, unable to stem the tide that pulled at her mind.

Gillian hissed, unable to contain the sound of pleasure as he nipped at the skin he uncovered. Tomi skated nearer to her center then danced away as she fisted her hands in the sheets, her heart pounding wildly. He did it again, each time closer to the very middle of her aching body.

"Tomi! Tomi! Don't stop!"

He didn't. Her eyes shut as tiny splintering explosions fired beneath her skin, all lit by her need for this man. His mouth settled over her and she let go of the world, her grip on reality spinning in a whirling vortex of pleasure and heat. The orgasm was strong, rippling through her as time seemed suspended. As reality impinged once more, she groaned. He didn't stop his torment. Tomi's tongue and mouth worked at her, wringing every ounce of satisfaction from her as she gasped for breath.

When Tomi raised his eyes to hers, they were slumber-ous, and very hungry. This man amazed her, from the deceptive strength of his body to his clever, quick mind. Now, he shared his passion as he crawled his way up her body.

"More. I want more. I want you, in every…possible… way." He dipped his mouth to her and on his lips she tasted her own essence. The musky tang mixed with the sweet, heady taste of Tomi. Bliss overwhelmed her and she was lost again as his hands grasped her nipples and softly tugged.

When he parted her legs once more, she accepted his direction gladly. She knew he would fill the emptiness that clawed inside her once more. His body, cradled to hers, was hard and hot, and she ached for him. The pressure of his shaft at her core stole what little breath remained in her body. She arched into him, needing him buried deep .

Then slowly, inch by slow, hungry inch, he entered her,

the sensation of stretching, of being one with him, nearly undid her. Tears leaked from the corners of her eyes as emotions battered her. Love. Need. *Hunger.*

"Don't cry, my love. I'd never hurt you," he whispered against her cheek, and surging emotions swelled in her heart.

"I'm crying, because I never... Ahhh!" She gulped. "I never thought... oh gods, Tomi! I never thought this day would come."

His hands traced over her cheek, brushing her skin with the pads of his fingertips before they moved on to cradle her head. He kissed her softly, but that lasted only seconds before it intensified and his mouth devoured her. She gave him everything. Including her very soul.

They moved. Rocked together. Neither of them spoke now in the hot confines of their pod. There were no words that could express pleasure as exquisitely as their tender touches or hungry movements. But when the climax took them, they were together. One being. Their arms and bodies intertwined. Then they slept.

Tomi woke slowly. He tried to turn, but the sting of cold metal at his back and a warm body nestled into him startled him.

"What?" As he opened his eyes, the memory rushed at him.

Gillian was in his arms and they were in the life pod. *We made love.* He smiled while reliving every second in his mind. It had been stronger—more intense—than anything he'd experienced before. That alone intrigued him as much as anything else. He'd never felt such completion before.

Never let go of himself like that with a woman. He hadn't wanted to give her less than his all.

A quick glance up told him they still had several hours left to wait. It would give him time to think and plan. Instinctively, his fingers threaded through hers as his eyes closed.

"Tomi?" She sounded groggy, as if sleep could steal her away once more.

"Yeah, I'm here." The rustling of sheets warned him that she had moved and he glanced in her direction. She'd turned so her eyes were in his direction.

"Where do we go now? I'm not… I don't believe in one-night stands." She spoke carefully, and he knew the risk she took in saying the words.

They gave him the power to hurt her. She wasn't a woman given to casual encounters. The deep well of honesty that she exuded had caught his attention from the beginning .

"No. I don't want that either. This…" He spread his hands and she remained silent. Watchful. "This was merely a beginning. I want to take you home with me. I want you at my side. My partner."

Her gaze shuttered. "I don't think there is any way this will work. I mean, I'm not someone you want to have around. Given my brother…"

He felt the icy cold wall lift between them once again and inwardly cursed. *I've rushed it.* "Don't borrow trouble, sweetheart. I certainly don't intend to." *I have to find some way to show her that we can be together.*

She levered up and away, tugging the sheet with her to cover her naked body. " Look, you're a senator and—"

"And you're the woman I love. So stop looking for outs, Gillian. If you want honesty, then by all means, let's be clear. I wanted you from the first time I saw you. But it wasn't right. You worked for me, so I never made a move. Now you don't. Not by my choice, but still—"

Gillian turned away in a single sharp move. "But here? This is just an interlude. It has to be."

The slow burn of anger rose in his chest. *Can't she see?* But of course, he knew she didn't understand. Her arrest, then dismissal, and the ignominy of her brother's crimes, had damaged the trusting part of her nature. It left her raw and distrustful.

He snatched at and caught her hand, bringing it to his now straining groin. "Does this feel like some bloody interlude to you?" He sighed, realizing that was a mistake immediately. A slow exhale helped him let go of some of the pressure in his chest. "While we're stuck in here we have an opportunity to talk. This? Between us? It's too..." He searched for the words.

"Maybe, we should check the status of the area?" She spoke quietly, and he reluctantly understood she needed space. It was true, too, that their situation right now was tenuous at best.

He tapped the communications tab as Gillian caught up her discarded clothing. "Status update on Vega II."

The light flashed green several times. "Vega II, status, controlled defense commenced. Captain Carmichael Snow in control. Base breach at sectors Alph a-Nine-Zeta and Beta-One-Zero-Gamma. Casualties, none known. Further information is classified."

What is Carmichael doing here? What brought him? And why didn't I know? But that was easy; he'd told his staff not to contact him unless it was an emergency requiring his vote.

"Communications, this is Senator Tomi Ito, override Alpha-Foxtrot-Mike-One-One-Zero. Voice activated." He waited as the computer checked his voiceprint against the records.

"Affirmative, Senator Tomi Ito. Request?" The tiny sound of the computer generated voice echoed in the small area.

"Current status of Vega II."

"Current Sit-Rep. Vega II under attack. Captain Carmichael Snow has reported five sublight destroyers. Total destroyed—three. Attack on Vega II continuing with insurgents in following zones—"

Tomi interrupted the modulated tones of the address system. "Override insurgent report."

"Recalibrating report. Unknown casualty rates. Some damage to life support systems on main level."

"Patch me through to Snow."

"Affirmative."

Tomi dragged a shaking hand through his hair. *Damage to life support could mean anything from ruptured oxygen tanks to a breach of the atmospheric dome. I need more information.* He caught Gillian's gaze, saw the way her eyes widened with fear. He reached out.

Gillian accepted the proffered hand and held on. The danger was so much more than he'd thought. He damned himself for not keeping her safe and tugged her into his arms. She came without demur.

"Tomi? Where the hell are you?" Carmichael, and he sounded angry.

"Yeah, it's me. I'm in a life pod, located—"

"No, on second thought, don't tell me where you are. I'm not sure how secure this connection is." A crackled sound of an exhalation echoed through the link. "You're okay though?"

Tomi frowned. "Yeah. Gillian is here with me. She says hi." In his arms, she wiggled but remained silent.

"Good. Stay safe, wherever you are. There are insurgents on Vega II hunting you. While you're in a secure tube, you should be fine." The words were a punch to his belly. Gillian straightened in his hold and tried to turn, but he kept her still.

"Really? Now isn't that interesting. Don't suppose you care to tell me why?"

"Not yet. But I have an idea. Just be ready to move if I have to find you." The babble of voices rose and fell in the background, and while Tomi couldn't make out the words, the tones were agitated. "Damn. I have to go. Just...just hang tight. Both of you."

The connection died away and there was almost silence, except for the sound of their breathing. *They're looking for me.*

Chapter 5

Gillian trembled and sat up. The Indy's were looking for Tomi and there wasn't anything she could do. She held her breath and focused on not screaming as fear crashed through her system. They were stuck in a life pod while the Indies looked for him. *I won't let them take him.* But what could she do? It wasn't like she had any kind of weapon, not unless she could somehow cobble something together from within this metal coffin. Her fingers curled.

"Gillian?"

She jumped, startled. "What?" Glancing up quickly, her head almost hit the roof of the tube in her haste. She spoke carefully, knowing now that so much depended on silence and hiding.

"You've tensed up on me. I didn't...I didn't hurt you, did I?"

A bubble of laughter rose in her throat. *Hysterical laughter.* She brutally tamped it down though. There was no time, and it certainly wasn't the place to give in to the rising panic. "No, Tomi. But we need to be quiet."

"I know, but I need you to know . Damn it, I care about you."

The ice around her heart melted a little at his words. They weren't quite the words she needed, but it was as close as it was going to get right now.

Her hand curved around his cheek, the gesture loving. "I know." She sucked in a long sigh. "We should rest for now."

He nodded, eyes stormy as he obviously weighed her words and actions. "For now. Later, we talk."

In silence, he assumed a prone position and she curled back down into his embrace, needing the reassurance of his closeness. It was only an interlude though , she reminded herself. Not long term. He had said he wanted her back, wanted everything, but he hadn't told her he loved her. And the specter of her brother still loomed. Tomi's hand traced lazy circles over her back and she drifted away.

It was the bang that woke her. "Stay still," Tomi whispered urgently in her ear, and her heart raced in fear.

Who is it? Carmichael and his people or the Indy's? The red emergency button above her glowed dully and she looked at Tomi. Had he done that? Tried to alert someone to their danger? He shook his head, as if he knew her thoughts.

A creak and a groan were followed by a large clang. It reverberated through the pod, echoing all the way to her stomach where it roiled like a writhing snake. She opened her mouth, but Tomi gave a quick motion of his head. She stilled her words. The enclosure shuddered.

Another clang erupted, and this time the emergency alarm in the capsule started to wail. "Breach of Life Support Systems."

Their hands joined, clung. Tomi squeezed tight and she accepted the modicum of reassurance.

Woosh! The door opened and before them, in old stained Indy uniforms, stood a ragtag group of soldiers.

"Get up! Get out!" The voice was loud and harsh. Her heart thudded in her throat.

Tomi climbed out, still naked, and she followed without grace. She wobbled slightly. Tomi gripped her wrist. One of the women eyed him up and down and Gillian had to stop herself from pushing in front of him. *He's mine!* Any such outburst wouldn't help right now, she knew.

"Cover yourself!" The man nearest them reached in, found Tomi's trousers, and thrust them at him.

Tomi released Gillian and stepped into the pants, but his broad, burnished chest shone under the dim lights. "Who are you, and where are you taking us?"

The man laughed brutally. "You'll be our prisoner, but your pretty friend? Well, I'm sure we could find a use—"

Tomi shoved forward. "You won't—"

A swift blunt end of a weapon in his solar plexus had him doubling over. Gillian stretched her hand toward him, but she was dragged back by her vicious captor.

"You're our prisoner. So shut up." The man jerked Gillian against him as she tried to move forward again.

She twisted and turned in his grip, but couldn't escape.

"I wouldn't do that, pretty one. Otherwise..." He let the threat hang in the air and tears formed in her eyes.

"Let him go and I'll give you—"

This time, the man uttered a harsh sound that was more like scratching fingernails on a slate surface. "I'll take what I want. I don't need you to give me anything." He tugged her against his body and revulsion rose as she felt the thickening of an erection at her hip. She strained away. His arm circled her waist, fingers splaying over her belly.

"Let her go." Tomi's voice was weak, and Gillian feared it was but the first of many injuries he'd sustain.

"Now that we have what we came for, we need to get out of here." Another voice, feminine in nature, called out.

"But the girl?" Another of his people spoke and her assailant cackled.

"He took my slave. I need another. She'll do perfectly." He slid his hand up and cupped Gillian's breast, squeezing hard, and she yowled, tugging away from his loathsome touch.

"Don't—" Tomi took another crack, this time across the back of his head. It felled him. The thud when he hit the floor echoed and Gillian cried out again.

"Pick him up. We can't afford to be caught."

Then she was tugged, slipping and fighting, to the lounge where she and Tomi had been about to settle in to eat. The man had her at the door, the slider open. He was shoving her forward when a voice called them to halt. She knew the voice. It was Carmichael.

He grabbed her ruthlessly, his arm now winding around her neck. "You want us? Then think about her!" The barrel of the laser pressed painfully into her side, digging into muscles and flesh. "I'll kill her, then it's his turn!"

Sweat formed on her face as she caught sight of naval officers waiting for them. Some were crouched behind conduit points and others stood, laser rifle to their shoulders, as if waiting for some order to shoot.

She was expendable. *But what about Tomi?* Was there

some way she could warn the officers? She sucked in a breath and screamed as fast and loud as possible. "Tomi Ito!"

A hand wound itself through her hair and pulled. "Argh!"

The pain was excruciating. Her knees gave out, and she dropped as the hand around her neck tugged again. She hoped it had been enough. Because there and then, she realized her time was over. It was too late. She just hoped it was enough to save him.

"I'll kill her!"

Behind them came a crashing sound. A whine split the air as another joined. A shock of pain ran through her. Then a gray curtain descended.

The action took place in slow motion for Tomi. One minute he was on his knees, shaking his head groggily and fending off the ache in his brain, then he was hauled upright. "Come with us now." He staggered through the doorway in time to see the man at the front stop. He'd been dragging Gillian to the door. Volcanic fury built inside Tomi. Boiling and ready to spew out, to burn everything within his path.

His words chilled Tomi to the marrow. "You want us? Then think about her!"

Tomi tugged against the hold on him. *Save Gillian!* The thought was primal—the need to save his mate, rising up. He tried to pull away, but savage hands and feet stopped him. He thudded once more to the floor, winded and in a mass of radiating pain.

He splayed his hands and attempted to push up, but a

foot landed on his back, holding him still with vicious pressure.

"Ugh!"

The blow was painful, and breathing was impossible without spikes of agony spreading through his chest.

"Let me up." *Get to Gillian! Don't let him take and hurt her!*

When Gillian screamed out his name, his chest nearly exploded with fear. *What the hell is she doing?* But he knew— his soul told him she would pay any price for his freedom. For an instant, he had to close his eyes. The pressure was too much. *I can't lose her now!*

"I'll kill her!"

The sound reverberated through his brain. *The bastard will too.* There was nothing left to lose. His brain spun as Tomi tried to think of some way he could stop her death. But he was supine on the floor, without a single weapon. Hope ebbed away, leaving him a cold and empty shell. Brittle.

A crash echoed and the sound of lasers deploying filled the air. The whine sharp as the condensed beam of light cut its path to whatever its target was. The man dropped to the floor, dead if the stench of burning flesh was anything to go by. Even as the pressure from the foot eased, Tomi was up and running. No one stopped him, though he dimly heard a babble of voices.

On the floor lay Gillian. *Pale. Still.* His heart cracked. *Dear gods! Don't let her be dead.*

His hands shook as he pushed her silky hair from her face. Only the slight rise and fall of her chest and the whisper of breath told him she still lived.

"Gillian." His voice broke as tears dripped down his

cheek. He wanted to gather her close, but without knowing the extent of her injuries…

She was alive, and he was thankful. Now, the muffled shouts and fighting behind him didn't exist. His whole being was centered on the woman in front of him. The one he hadn't ever told of his love. The cold reality was that she was much too good for him. She had an inner well of strength. And how he wished he could call upon it right now, when he needed it the most.

"Gillian, can you hear me?" Tomi raised his head as a gentle hand was laid on his shoulder.

"Is she…" Carmichael squatted beside him.

"She's alive. But I don't…" He couldn't finish the words. It hurt far too much.

"I need a medic here!" Carmichael bellowed, and Tomi felt insignificant and useless. A woman scurried over and dropped beside Gillian. "Let me in so I can check her." She had a tiny medi-scanner in her hand. Slowly, she waved it over Gillian, and Tomi waited, the not knowing clawing at him. With a sigh, she rocked back on her knees. "She needs urgent medical attention."

Carmichael nodded. "Arrange a team to get her to my ship." Then he pulled his brother-in-law away whilst a group of people fashioned a board to carry her on. Tomi moved to help and Carmichael held him back. "My men are trained for this. Let them do their job."

So Tomi did, his gaze dogging their every move. Then they hoisted her up and she was gone. Taking his heart with her. "She needs…" His hand reached out, but Carmichael gripped his shoulders, shaking him. Stopping him from following.

"Right now she needs medical help. The best place to deal with her injuries is on my ship." Tomi wanted to argue, but Carmichael shook his head. "Tomi, we need to talk."

He didn't want to. Hell, he wanted to go with Gillian, but he didn't even know where they'd taken her—what path they took—just that she was out of his sight. "I don't…"

"This was a setup, Tomi. They were after you. My men got wind of it, which is why I'm here."

Tomi stiffened then turned and looked at the large man who was frowning at him. "Just what do you mean by that?"

"I mean—"

"Sir! We need you over here." A woman, slender and young, called to Carmichael, her face grave. "You're going to want to see this."

Tomi watched as Carmichael swung away. He'd muttered a harsh epithet as his feet moved swiftly. A knot of officers crowded around and a rapid-fire conversation ensued. At the end, the scowl etched on his friend's face told him the news wasn't good.

"Tomi, we have to get you out of here, now. Come on."

Carmichael grabbed him, moving at a rapid clip out the door.

Oh gods! How I ache! Coming to wasn't pleasant, as the throb in Gillian's side told her something had happened. Her mouth felt like dry sandpaper and breathing was painful indeed. Opening her eyes reminded Gillian that she wasn't in the pod with Tomi. In fact, she really didn't know where she was.

Cracking her eyes open a little was hard, as the lethargy of whatever they'd given her hadn't totally worn off, she guessed. "Where… Where am I?"

"Yes, I thought you might be waking soon."

Gillian laid both hands flat as if to rise.

"No, stay right where you are. Can't have you undoing all my hard work, now can we?" The voice was cheerful and Gillian scowled.

"Where's Tomi? Where am I?" Panic set in. Great big, greasy waves washed through her.

"Senator Ito is just outside. Don't stress, otherwise your blood pressure will spike and I'll have to keep you here longer."

She wanted to lash out, but her rational mind urged her to be cautious. After all, she still wasn't sure as to her location, and clearly the man standing in front of her had no intention of telling her.

"So how soon can I get out of here? Wherever here is?"

He grinned as she controlled an outburst of temper. "Well, my dear, since you seem so inclined to leave us, I would think in a few minutes you should be able to go."

He must have seen the confusion she felt, telegraphed on her face. "You're on the *Emancipation*. In the medical wing. Now, I'll send the senator in, but before you go, some advice. Getting too active for the next few days is inadvisable. You had a nasty laser wound, which I have spent the last two days repairing. The skin has knitted together nicely, as have the muscles and organs, but I don't want you back here because you've torn anything."

Heat crept over her skin. He thought she was going to go have sex with Tomi—Senator Ito? "Yeah, I promise to stay quiet."

He gazed at her, his face alive with curiosity and she nearly ducked. "Fine, then. I'll go get him." The man trudged to the end of the bed, opened the narrow door, and dipped his head around. "You can come in now."

Tomi appeared at the doorway, his face drawn and hair messy. "Gillian!" His rapid footsteps brought him to the side of her bed, where he caught both her hands up in his. She noted dimly that they shook.

"She needs quiet, Senator. I'm going to release her into your care as discussed. However, I don't want her excited or upset. And I'll need to see her again when we reach Reunion."

Tomi nodded. "Of course. How soon can I…"

"Well, she'll no doubt wish to dress, but after she's done that, you can escort her to her berth. But she must rest. I'll be checking on that." The medic gave them a benign smile and a lump formed in Gillian's throat. He was wrong. *Tomi and I…* There was no *them*.

"She'll be with me."

The medic gave Tomi a last long look, then nodded.

"I'm fine. Just find me a cabin."

The look Tomi gave her stopped her from speaking again. Hot and full of some deep, dark emotion, it was almost too much to bear, because it wasn't some pale emotion she saw there in his eyes. No. But there could never be anything between them now. He was a senator and she, merely the sister of a felon. Surely he could see that?

"You'll come with me once you're dressed." His words sounded final, and she sighed. He turned on his heel and left the cabin.

"You know, I really—"

"Miss Edgemont, you should trust the senator. He's

dogged my door for the last two days that you've been here."

For a moment, she was sure he was going to say something more before he shrugged. "I've put fresh clothes here on the chair and I believe your belongings have been transferred to the ship."

The door closed silently behind him and she slumped back down to the bed. "What am I supposed to do?" But there was no answer in the quiet room.

Pulling back the sheets and sliding to the edge of the bed was a trial as her side tugged and ached. She carefully dressed, and a look in the mirror showed a fright of a woman with bed hair and deep bruises under her eyes. So much for Tomi seeing her at her best.

She looked around, but no shoes were evident, just a set of slippers, and she slid her feet within, all the while wishing for a hairbrush and a denta-tab to remove the sour taste from her breath.

"Well, I guess this is as good as it gets." She made for the door and felt foolish as Tomi welcomed her with a grin.

Tomi felt a surge of elation pumping through his veins. He didn't plan on taking Gillian to any other cabin than his own, because there was so much he needed to tell her. That she was both alive and on the road to recovery were gifts. He took her hand with great tenderness. "We'll go slowly."

He led her down the corridor, keeping a close eye on her. Toward the end of the walk, she was pale and a little unsteady. *If only I could carry her.* But he knew she wouldn't accept that. Not yet, anyway. His Gillian would make some pithy comment, the steel spine he knew she had would straighten, and her face would assume that don't -touch-me look she'd perfected.

At the cabin, she sank into the chair, hissing slightly. The white room was soulless, but for once he was pleased, because it was also private. The soft leather armchairs were laid out in a circle. Gillian took the one closest to the door.

"Would you like a drink?"

She gave him an assessing look. "This is your cabin?"

A blush crawled over his skin, hot and prickly. "Yeah."

Her face assumed a cold shuttered look. "Look, what we had—"

He lifted his hand, knowing that he had to stop her before she said something they would both regret. "We can talk about that in a minute. Right now, I need a drink, and I'm guessing you do too."

He turned away, grateful for a chance to compose himself. On her face, he saw the distance she was trying to put between them. He couldn't allow that. Not now. *Not when I've tasted paradise.*

Tomi poured two drinks, a peppermint tea for her—her favorite, he remembered—and a whiskey for himself. *Before this is done, I'm going to need some fortification.* He turned back to her with a smile and popped the cup on the small table beside her seat. He chose the seat opposite her.

"So, what now? What happened to…" She stopped, paled a little further, and his heart ached for her.

"We got them. But…" There was so much he had to say to her. *How do I tell her? Where do I even begin?*

Her green eyes shone with tears and he would banish them, if only she'd let him. But not yet. He hadn't told her everything. *A clean slate to start with.*

"So what? What's with the 'but'?" White lines bracketed her mouth.

"There are things that have come to light. Things that none of us expected. Gillian…" He rose, unable to tell her the truths sitting down. He was wired. "I… Your brother…"

She surged up, gasping and clutching her side.

Tomi wanted to recoil as she flinched. "No, he hasn't done anything. Your brother was a deep undercover agent. None of us knew." The words spilled out and she swayed in his arms.

"What?" She sank back to the seat.

"Carmichael received an encoded communiqué while we were down on the surface. After you were shot. We had to hurry back here." His much vaunted oratory skills eluded him. Now, when everything hung on his words, they fled.

"He's undercover?"

Tomi squatted beside her as she closed her eyes. Her hand fluttered over her mouth as if holding in the tide of emotions. A sob wracked her frame, and she wrapped her other arm around herself. *Fragile.* She looked like the slightest breeze would shatter her. A single tear traced down her pale cheek. Tomi would have given anything right now to spare her any further pain.

"Gillian, the plot against Kumi was a setup. He'd hoped to stop it before it happened, but his mission was to worm his way into the Indy camp and find out who was leading them. It was all part of a plan. Then when things went sour, he had to go along with it. It was necessary for him to take the fall, so it didn't compromise all his work."

Gillian shook her head. "I don't understand. What are you saying?"

"He's being released later today. Exonerated."

Her eyes, deep wells of sparkling emerald stared back at him. "So he's…"

"He only carried out his orders."

"And Carmichael. He never knew? Is that right, Tomi?"

Tomi shook his head. "No. And now you know. Sweetheart—"

"Don't. Don't start with that sweetheart stuff. I'm not…" Gillian reached out both hands, entreating him to stop.

Her words sliced through him. "Why? Because you don't want to hear it?" Anger bubbled over. "Well, that's too bad. Because I have to tell you."

Once more, Gillian flinched at his words. *"Please."*

"Listen to me, Gillian. When you were shot, I felt like my guts had been ripped out. The pain… It was too much. Seeing you lying there, I realized then, you could be gone in an instant, and I…I couldn't believe I'd been so blind. You'd been there, in my arms, where you belonged, and not once…" He had to stop, hand on his chest, banishing the remembered pain and anguish coursing through him. "Not ever, did I tell you how I felt. I was a coward."

His chest bellowed. Talking from the heart like this didn't come easily, but he'd tear his emotions to shreds if only she'd listen. If only she'd accept his words. Because every one was true. Every one was honest.

"What? What?" Her voice shook and he hoped, dear gods, he prayed it meant she too was almost overcome by her emotions.

"I love you. I have for a long time."

Gillian coughed and snorted, her hands rising to her face in embarrassment. "Oh gods!"

"What?" Now that he'd bared his soul, he waited. *Surely…*

"You have the worst timing of anyone I know. You should have told me before!"

Bewilderment filled him. *What do her words mean?* He needed her to respond. He couldn't do any more. So he watched her and waited for her words.

A blink sent a single diamond-like tear trickling down her cheek. "Damn it, Tomi, I love you too."

"Well…" He huffed, his chest full of pride. "Well, that's great. Now let's talk about getting married."

Chapter 6

The ship was little more than a blip in the dark night, the shuttle speeding toward the surface of Gillian and Tomi's home. Reunion. There was something in the name, she mused. Her fingers were wound through Tomi's. He squeezed, as if he understood the introspective thoughts. "When we get home—"

"Your brother will be there, together with Kumi, Renjiro, and Selina. It's a shame your parents couldn't get away."

She sighed and shifted in her seat. "I'm kind of glad, right now. I feel like we need to have some kind of closure on the mess. I mean, with Kumi and Anderson." She broke off. *How can I possibly explain how it felt?* He was her twin brother and the victim had been Tomi's sister.

"Prepare for landing." The carefully modulated voice broke through her thoughts. Pulling her hands away, Gillian braced herself, the way she usually did against the seat, taking deep breaths as the ground rushed up to meet them.

The landing thrusters engaged with a whine and their

speed slowed until they hovered above the asphalt surface. Then, with a gentle kiss, they touched down. The sound of snicks filled the air as everyone rushed to release their safety harnesses. She chanced a look out the portal and there he was...her brother.

Tomi took her hand once more and led her from the small ship. They made their way over the surface to the fence. Then they were through the gate. Anderson stepped in front of her and for a moment they stared at each other. Then she launched. "You big foolish glom!"

The feel of him wrapping her in his arms felt good. "I'm sorry, Gillian. I couldn't tell you."

She tugged away and patted his face. "I understand. Well, at least now. Look, you need to meet—"

"The senator. Sir, I don't know how..." Anderson was uneasy. It was clear in the way he danced from one foot to the other.

Tomi shook his hand. "It's done. We won't ever speak of it again."

Gillian stopped herself from rolling her eyes. *Men! The old, it's-done-and-no-more-emotional-outbursts is really a bit old.* She glanced over Anderson's shoulder, watching as Carmichael greeted his tiny partner, Kumi. The way their arms were wrapped around each other was intimate yet open. "We should —"

"Yes, sweetheart. Anderson have you met my sister?" Tomi's voice sent Anderson blushing. He hadn't yet got over his welcome, it seemed.

"Not really, no. But I doubt—"

Gillian grabbed her brother's hand. "Come on, she's great." While Anderson quirked his eyebrow at her, she tugged him along toward the embracing couple.

"I don't think..."

Gillian stopped and Tomi barreled into her, slipping his hand around her waist. "Everything okay, sweetheart?"

She grinned at the look of disbelief on her brother's face. "You're just both going to have to get over your embarrassment with each other, because Tomi and I... Well, we're going to get married. And I need you and Kumi to get along."

Anderson's smile wobbled a little. "Well, damn. I'm willing to try, if Madam Kumi is."

Anderson was greeted by Kumi with a cool reception. Gillian was sure it would warm over time. But it was Kumi's enthusiasm at their news that lifted whatever dark cloud might still have been marring their news. "I knew it! When I contacted you…"

Tomi gave her a mock frown. "Yes, I heard about that. You and I are going to have to chat."

Kumi laughed. "You both just needed a little push in the right direction. I always knew you were meant to be together!"

Gillian laughed at her words. Kumi was right. She and Tomi were meant to be together. Kumi waved their official vehicles forward and Gillian turned to Anderson. "How did you get here?"

"I used an air-taxi."

"Ha! Tomi?" She turned and he smiled. The look was indulgent, she thought. "Come on, you're coming with us."

The three of them climbed into Tomi's vehicle which pulled up in front of them. Tomi gave directions to Kumi and Carmichael's house then he settled back, silently sinking into the seats. Gillian looked out the window. So much had changed, yet outside everything looked the same. "What happened to—"

"When we get to Kumi and Carmichael's, sweetheart.

Then we can discuss it." Tomi's words reminded her that she would need to learn to mind her words around others. She snuggled in, savoring the feeling of elation. Two of the most important men in her life, Anderson and Tomi, were there with her. It was both surreal and uplifting.

Kumi met them at the gate and ushered them all in. They settled in the office where Gillian had watched Tomi talking to Kumi the fateful night of the abduction. Tomi's cousin, Renjiro, and his wife, Selina, joined them soon after, making themselves at home on one of the sofas against the wall. There was an air of expectancy and Gillian couldn't help herself.

"Where is she?" She looked for the girl who'd been known as *slave*.

"We managed to find her family through DNA typing. They have taken responsibility for her care. We'll keep tabs on her." Kumi shrugged. "But she needed to go home. By the way, she did have a name. Chastity. It's quite ironic that she was actually a runaway who'd been prostituting herself when she was taken prisoner."

Gillian looked at Tomi and shook her head. "I was jealous, you know. I thought you and she…" She stared at him, once again surprised at the depths of his love for her. She saw it shining in his eyes.

Tomi wrapped his arms around her. "Never. I felt responsible for what happened to her. But you were always the one for me." He dropped a tiny kiss on her forehead before swiveling in his brother-in-law's direction. "Now, Carmichael, what's the status of things?"

"The man we shot? He was the head of the Indies. Duvall St. Justice." Carmichael turned to address Anderson. "He's the one you were after."

Anderson inclined his head. "I was as close as I'd ever been when things went wrong. He was charismatic enough that he could hold most of them together. I was starting to hear things . Well, up until the attack on Madam Kumi. Then St. Justice let Dobry take the fall. He headed for cover and, for a while, I was sure my mission was a total failure."

Carmichael nodded. "I know that you were acting under orders, but I need to clear the air right now. If she'd died, you'd be dead."

Anderson nodded, his face grave. "I understand."

"So, the latest update is that, with St. Justice eliminated, the Indy's are in disarray. Unfortunately for them, he'd neutralized any possible successor as each one popped up. The fleet will continue mopping up the mess, but word is those we caught are singing any song they can to minimize their incarceration. It'll take some time, but we believe the Federation is finally safe." Carmichael stilled, his pleasure clear from the grin on his face. "Selina and Ren, your child should enjoy a period of unprecedented peace."

Renjiro and his wife smiled.

It had almost all gone so wrong. Gillian couldn't control the shiver at the thought. "All right?" Tomi whispered in her ear as she snuggled into his embrace.

"Yeah. Everything is finally all right."

The chirruping of crickets filled the air. "So where exactly are we?" Gillian followed Tomi along the path lit with tiny lanterns.

"It's my family's private retreat. No one comes here

much anymore. It seemed like the right place to enjoy our private honeymoon."

Gillian couldn't hold back the smile. Today had been perfect. Long and exhausting, but perfect. Everyone important to them had attended their formal wedding ceremony. But now it was just them.

Ahead loomed a wood house. It wasn't overly large, but it possessed a veranda that wrapped around the front and an air of happiness.

"I spent many summers here. It's where I learned to sail, and we had the freedom to come and go without scrutiny." Tomi fished around in his pockets. "Ah, here it is. Now, Mrs. Ito, come here and give your husband a kiss."

A thrill shot through her. *Mrs. Ito.* It still seemed fantastical to her. She leaned in and he kissed her. The heat in that caress shot fire through her. When he gathered her close, she didn't demur. His lips ravished hers and when he lifted her, she held on, lost in the thrall of passion.

He pulled away and grunted. "I just need to get the door."

"Well, you could put me down."

He smiled. The tender look filled her with emotion. "I read about this ancient custom of a groom carrying his bride over the threshold. It seems appropriate." His hands fiddled with the lock for a moment before entering silently. He took a couple of steps into the room. It was welcoming and casual. In her mind, it was the Tomi that very few saw. The private man.

Slowly, he lowered her to the floor, their bodies touching as she slid down. Now she was ready for the raging hunger that had stayed banked all day.

The kiss turned hot. Their mouths clung and tongues danced while hands roamed. The hardness of the wall barely made an impact on her thoughts as he pushed her back. When he found the sweet spot of her neck she arched into him. "Tomi!"

"Your outfit is lovely, but right now, I'd prefer you naked." His rasping words sent a shiver of expectation and her core pulsed with need.

Her breathless laugh was swallowed by another kiss. One that scorched, and fires licked at her skin. The heat grew. They pulled away, breathless.

Her fingers found zippers and buttons, shedding the jacket of her fine silk suit while he discarded his own clothing. It pooled on the floor, forgotten.

A momentary stab of consciousness prevailed as a tiny breeze kissed her skin. "The door!"

He kicked it closed and she dropped her pants to where they joined her shirt. In bra and panties, she surveyed the glorious sight before her. His body, firm, rigid, and naked, was bathed in moonlight. The bronze of his skin kissed with silvery white moonbeams. Truly, he looked like a god. As she started to slip the straps of her bra off, he stopped her.

"No. Let me."

With tenderness, he slipped his long fingers under the strap, toyed for a moment while she gasped, then trailed them over her shoulders and down her back.

"You skin is finer than silk. So soft. So perfect." His words drugged her. So deep and intense was the timbre of his tone that she shook.

His gaze caught hers, captured her like a spider in his web. His fingers found the clasp and released her, she felt the sag of her breasts, and the air teased her nipples into tighter, aching buds of desire.

She pushed against him, needing the touch of skin to skin, and where they touched she burned.

"Please." The word was little more than a whimper.

"Soon, sweetheart. It isn't a race." But the teasing words were strained and she knew he too felt the hunger. The desire. The need.

When his fingers found the lacy edge of her panties, her knees nearly buckled. With care, he pushed them away, down her legs , before he stepped back. "My goddess. Come with me, Gillian."

He held out his hand and she took it, prepared to follow him to the ends of the universe. Tomi led her through the house, and in the center was an immense bedroom. The four-poster in the middle was festooned with white gauzy curtains and flower petals decorated the coverlet.

When he gently pushed her down, she let him.

His eyes glittered in the glow coming from the domed skylight above the bed. Then he was there, covering her. His fingers toyed with her belly, slipping gently over it with a reverence that stole her breath. "I'm going to fill you. I'm going to plant myself deep within you and, I hope, create something new. Something of us."

Her heart lurched. She too wanted that.

The whisper of his words, sliding over naked skin, drove thought from her mind. He caressed his way down her abdomen and to her core, leaving her reeling with sensual overload. Gillian curled her fingers in the material. She needed him. Wanted him. Loved him.

As he probed, his lips found a breast. He suckled and she arched up again , needing all of him. "Tomi!" She nearly splintered there, but he teased her unmercifully. Kisses, nibbles, and sucks interspersed with tender words.

"Not yet, sweetheart. Feel the burn. Let it grow."

Her hands reached up to grasp his shoulders and gripped the hard flesh. "Now, Tomi! No more. Come to me!" This time, he didn't retreat, and her heart raced, sweat shined on their bodies. And she crooned, "I need you. Fill me."

His lips fastened on the skin at her neck once more while she rocked and entreated. He settled himself at the cradle of her hips, the thick head of his erection notched between the lips of her sex. A gentle nudge. No more.

She gasped. Eyes closing while above her, he panted. He shook, straining she knew to build the pleasure to hold on. *Too much! Not enough!* She felt the slide of his cock as she sheathed him. Heat and light assaulted her senses, and their mouths met.

He moved and so did she. Together. Give and take warred until finally, the precipice loomed. Pressure grew deep inside her belly until finally, she let go, feeling her body explode in a million pieces of pleasure. He joined her, his cry of fulfillment loud in the near silence.

When they stilled, holding onto each other in the night-light, she smiled. "I give you my forever, Tomi."

He sealed the vow with a kiss.

Levia scanned the long line of other hopefuls entering the testing chamber. The large building in the center of town was cold, and she dragged her wrap around her body, even as she craned her head, looking to the high ceiling. She'd never before had an occasion to enter the testing complex, yet she'd seen the lines of teenagers every time they passed the building.

Once she'd asked her parents why the teens were lined up and her mother's face had shuttered. Her stepfather had just shaken his head and growled. They'd stopped her questions with a carefully uttered, "You'll know soon enough, Levia." The pain in her mother's eyes had been enough to shush her questions. For endless months afterward, her parents had traveled different routes to the educational facility she attended and Levia lost interest in the puzzle of that building.

Now, as she looked around, remembering that long ago spring day, it was her opportunity to find out. But she felt a surge of concern at what lay ahead. She likely wasn't the only one, given that there were probably two to three hundred seventeen-year-olds gathered in the one place. Ahead of her, she caught sight of a couple of girls, their arms linked together and wide smiles on their faces. Scanning the crowd, she became aware that, by far, a majority of those gathered displayed both fear and trepidation.

"All female subjects will enter through doors three, six, and seven. All male subjects will enter through gates four, eight, and ten." The speaker above her was loud, and she jumped before checking the numbers etched on the black metal sign over her head.

The massive doors beside her swung open, and now an uncertain silence reigned. Many of the youngsters hung back, clearly discomforted by whatever testing regime lay ahead. This was where they'd been told their futures would be determined.

"Oh gosh, I hope they only have an aptitude and psych eval. I don't think..." Levia turned to see the white face of the girl behind her. The girl had uttered what many must silently be thinking.

Levia dragged an unsteady breath in, her hand resting flat against the plane of her belly as she looked around. No one had entered yet. It was clear many were on the verge of taking the step, but still they hung back.

She straightened her shoulders. "I'm not afraid." It was always wiser to approach things head-on, she believed. When her biological father had died, she'd been one of the few to view his capsule before it was sent into the massive gray structure built to accommodate those who'd moved onto the next life realm.

Her legs shook as she wobbled toward the entrance. Beyond the doorway, she spied sealed cubicles and her heart stuttered. Why cubicles? Usually testing—med and psych—were in eval-units, hidden only by billowing white curtains. She glanced back, noting that others had taken the first step.

"Move along, subjects." Once again, the androgynous voice of the address system blared.

Of course, given it was her seventeenth anniversary of birth, she was technically considered an adult now.

She thought longingly of baby Rald and her half-sister, Elda, waiting at home for her to return, and the celebrations to be held that night. That made her smile. She would need to make them proud of her.

She entered a row and the tall Educational Specialist, the edu-specs as her peers laughingly called them, stopped her. "Present your credentials to the scanner."

She'd done this many times since the tiny implant had been slipped below the dermal layer of her skin at birth. The small unit in her wrist heated as her details were checked.

"Enter the first cubicle, Levia Endrado, and follow the instructions to complete your assessment."

Thus dismissed, Levia moved to the first unit, laid her

palm against the scanner, and the door slid open soundlessly.

"Welcome, Levia Endrado. Take your place in the eval-unit." The soft contralto of the voice echoed after the door closed silently behind her.

"What are you evaluating?" Her voice was breathy, and she peered around.

"Your skills—physical and psychological. Your emotional and medical status. Your educational attainment levels."

It was an answer that shed little insight into the many things she was hungry to know. "Why do all seventeen year olds—" "Take a seat, Levia. Then we may begin your testing." If she'd expected an answer, she was sadly mistaken, she considered sourly. She dropped into the seat, the soft leather-like surface molding to her body. "Levia Endrado, you are required to remove all non-specified apparel." She jolted in the chair. "It's cold." "The temperature will be amended. Remove the non-specified apparel." Her misgivings grew as she dragged off the light wrap she'd brought with her, and then threw it to the floor at the side of the unit. "We will begin, Levia Endrado. At any time, should you experience any malfunctions of the unit, simply depress the red button." It glowed and she grimaced. Levia reclined against the chair and waited for the testing to begin. The first examination was based on her understanding of the political system, where she saw herself, and her knowledge of the rights and responsibilities accorded through citizenship of both her planet and the commonwealth.

The second test was mathematical and scientific proficiency. It felt like hours had passed by the time she'd finished, and she lay limp on the seat, exhausted.

"Levia Endrado, you may rise. The sanitary unit will emerge once you trigger the yellow button at the door. Should you require refreshment, press the blue button and a restorative will be made available."

"Can I leave?" "Negative, Levia Endrado. Your needs will be catered for in this capsule." "Why?" Her voice hitched and true fear rose for the first time. Why did they keep her in the alcove? "All will be revealed at the end of the testing cycle." Levia looked at the now empty screen before hurling a curse word. It was met with silence. The urgent throb of her bladder reminded her that she needed to use the facilities, so, with

a sigh, she rose and clambered from the seat. After attending to the needs of her body, she walked around the unit, peering at the door, but it was obviously programmed remotely. She poked and prodded, but it made no differ-ence. With a huff, she headed back to the chair.

The moment she'd settled in, the viewing screen shone bright. "Welcome back, Levia. The next sequence will evaluate your psychological reflexes, then that will be followed up with the general knowledge portion of the evaluation."

"When can I leave?" It seemed better to ask bluntly, she told herself.

"Once the examination is completed. After the next set of evaluations, you will be subjected to the physical aspect."

"Then I can go home?"

"Levia Endrado, you will now complete the psycholog-ical test. This will be undertaken by one of the center's personal evaluators."

She frowned. Personal evaluators? She bit her lip, and the sting reminded her that this wasn't something to joke about. In her seventeen years, she'd only heard of personal evaluators being brought in once before, and that was when one of the girls at her academy had been in a serious accident. Both legs were amputated and her body's ability to keep her alive had been gravely compromised. Her peers had been informed that the girl had requested the assessment before she could request her support systems be disconnected.

"Levia Endrado, are you ready to recommence processing?" The emotionless voice echoed once more and she gulped.

"Yes."

Available from Beachwalk Press
http://www.beachwalkpress.com

Direct Autographed Books
http://bit.ly/BioCybe

Starline by Imogene Nix

Duvall McCord stepped out of line as the parade was dismissed, inwardly wincing as his new boots rubbed his feet and his new uniform scratched his neck. He looked at his

family, considering and measuring. He'd worked hard to attain the grades needed to be able to enter the academy, but it was all he'd ever wanted and dreamed of. To travel the stars and eventually captain his own ship. Now there he was on the cusp. Even as a fosterling, his room had been decorated with the ships he one day wanted to command, and at the age of twenty-three he was finally on the way.

His father, Captain Gentry, who had given up the chance of a plum command to keep his family happy, was always in the back of his mind. He now captained inter-galaxy runs for the Admiralty. He'd even given up his Star Destroyer for his wife's peace of mind. Duvall promised himself he'd never do that.

He belonged somewhere out there, among the biggest, the boldest, and the best.

His little sister, Meredith, bounced up and down, squeaking excitedly, and his parents smiled. He felt their genuine fondness for him, their foster son. They were proud of his many achievements, and if there were doubts in their minds, they were never spoken of.

Duvall was driven, almost obsessive in his desire to become the best of the best. That was why, now at the end of his time in the academy, he had been nominated as Best of his Class. The Top Graduate. The one his peers looked up to. The question had been asked and answered: was he good enough? His answer was always an unequivocal "yes." His family, peers, and instructors saw the drive and accepted it for what it was—an integral part of who he was. His mentor, Captain Gustav Elphin, had requested that

he serve aboard the Star of Ishtar, and had taken a great personal interest in this cadet.

It was acknowledged he would be on the fast-track to the stars. And, as Elphin told him again and again, emotional entanglements grounded a man; a piece of advice Duvall took seriously, so he had been careful in his social encounters. Always keeping a light touch with his lovers. Love 'em and leave 'em was his motto. He refused to let anything get in the way of his achievements and the desire to captain his own ship.

If privately his parents had any doubts about his lack of emotional ties to the women he was seen with, they kept them to themselves. No doubt they believed that one day a woman would change his mind and the attitude he had worked so hard to foster. For now, he accepted their belief that he knew what he wanted and had the drive to achieve it.

War was finally over and there was time to settle down. Long days of peace stretched out before them. The uneasy truce between the Earth Empire and the Ru'Edan, while new and tenuous, meant that there were opportunities diplomatically for the right kind of man and woman.

The rogue Admiral of the Ru'Edan Empire, Crick Sur Banden, might still be on the loose, but there was a belief that soon he would be brought to ground and that a true peace might be the outcome. Well, that was the opinion of the hopeful in the Empire anyway. The Empire held its collective breath as the newest graduates of the Earth Empire Academy marched out. They hoped to reap the benefits of those who came before.

Available from Beachwalk Press
http://www.beachwalkpress.com

Direct Autographed Copy
http://bit.ly/StarlineNix

Cyborg: Redux by Imogene Nix

Once evil reigns there is only the honest left to fear...

Clarissa was an ordinary nanny until Dr. Jeremy Colvert made her a bio cybernetic freak. On the run, it was an act of kindness that nearly brought her undone.

When Michael met Clarissa everything in his world changed—again. Now they're hiding from a world out to get them and the aim to shut down Dr. Colvert's experimentation isn't exactly going to plan.

Love might have bloomed, but there'll be no future if they can't save each other.

Inheritance Of the Blood by Imogene Nix

In this place it was always better not to know.

In the darkness evil waits...

As a young bride Kira was whisked away from everything and everyone she knew, including her new husband and became Christina, an operative of the Displaced Persons Unit.

As the danger grows she sees an opportunity to save her husband Vasya and sister Serina. But nothing is the same. Serina is grown up—married and pregnant.

Vasya too is older and darkly forbidding. Trusting Christina doesn't come easily until a catastrophic event takes place. Now, knowing the truth everything he thought he knew is changed. But at a very high cost.

The four must work together to defeat the Demon, Zuor and the stakes are higher than they imagined and all could be lost.

Also by Imogene Nix

Warriors of the Elector

Star of Ishtar

Starline

Starfire

Star of the Fleet

Starburst

Star of Eternity

Blood Secrets

The Blood Bride

The Illuminated Witch

The Sorcerer's Touch

Reunion Trilogy

War's End

The Assassin

Executing Justice

Sex Love & Aliens

Tangled Webs

False Webs

Covert Webs

21st Testing Protocol

Cyborg: Redux (December 2017)

Children Of A Greater Evil (2018)

<u>Single Titles</u>

The Chocolate Affair

A Sapphire for Karina

The Plan

BioCybe

Hesparia's Tears

Tomorrow's Promise

A Bar In Paris

Blame The Wine

A Stranger's Embrace

Revenge On Cupid

Inheritance Of The Blood

<u>Non Fiction</u>

Self Publishing: Absolute Beginners Guide (With Suzi Love)

About the Author

Imogene is published in a range of romance genres including Paranormal, Science Fiction and Contemporary. She is mainly published in the UK and USA due to the nature of her tales.

In 2011, Imogene Nix was born in Bondi, NSW during a Romance Readers Convention. From there, there was no stopping her! Imogene sat down and worked tirelessly for 3 months culminating in the books Starline. This book became the first in a trilogy titled, "Warriors of the Elector."

Imogene has successfully been contracted for twenty-five titles and self published three others, under this pseudonym. She has also completed another three and is, like many of her contemporaries, seeking homes for these books—with at least one likely to be self published once ready.

Imogene is and has been a member of a range of

professional organisations, including Romance Writers of Australia, (ARRA) Australian Romance Readers Association, Science Fiction Romance Brigade (SFRB), Dark Siders Down Under (the Australian Paranormal, Erotic Writers of Australia, (ALLi) Alliance of Independent Authors, Queensland Writers Centre and most recently Romance Writers of New Zealand.

She also mentors new writers and love to drink coffee, wine & eat chocolate and is parenting 2 spoiled dogs and a ferocious cat!

To contact Imogene

www.imogenenix.net
imogene@imogenenix.net